LOVE'S MAGIC

LOVE'S MAGIC BOOK 1

BETTY MCLAIN

This book is dedicated to all the people who believe in the magic of love.

PROLOGUE

"Yes," Mallie agreed. She took the hand he extended and allowed herself to be pulled to her feet. They walked back, slowly, holding hands, enjoying being together. When they stopped and turned to face each other, Daniel leaned forward and gave Mallie a gentle kiss. Mallie felt her toes curl into the sand. She looked down in surprise.

"I don't have any shoes on," she said in surprise. She looked at Daniel's feet. "You don't either."

Daniel looked down and grinned. "I guess we didn't think we needed them," Daniel replied. "When I decided I wanted to go to the beach, I just thought about pants and a shirt, and suddenly I was wearing them. I never thought about shoes until you mentioned them."

"I didn't either. I wonder if we are getting sand on our hospital sheets." Mallie laughed at the thought.

"I don't think so. I think that we are only here in spirit." Daniel said sadly.

CHAPTER 1

The machines were all beeping and showing red squiggly lines as the lady sat in the chair beside the bed. She was holding tightly onto the hand of her daughter, who was hooked up to the machines. There were tears running down her cheeks, but she made no effort to stop them, other than a swipe with the back of her hand every once in a while.

"Oh, Mallie," She cried. "Why did this have to happen to you?" She gazed at her beautiful daughter, whose face was bruised from the accident. Malinda had been riding her scooter home from class at the college, when a car came around a corner and hit her. The young boy, who had been driving the car, failed to see the scooter until it was too late. The boy was not hurt, but Malinda was in a coma. The doctors were doing a series of tests to see how badly she was hurt. So far there was nothing conclusive.

The nurse came into the room to check on the machines. She looked at Dana Wilson sitting by her daughter's side, holding her hand, and silently crying. She shook her head. She felt very sorry for Mallie's mother. It is always harder on the parents, especially when an accident takes them by surprise. She quietly put a hand on the mother's shoulder.

"Mrs. Wilson, why don't you take a short break? You can walk around, maybe go down to the cafeteria and get something to eat." The nurse encouraged.

"No, I am fine." Dana sat up straighter to prove she was alright. She was feeling every one of her forty-six years at that moment.

The nurse sighed, but didn't press her.

"If you need anything let me know," she replied.

"Thank you, I will." Dana replied.

After the nurse left, Dana started thinking about the life she and Mallie had lived. It was just the two of them and it had been that way for the last ten years, since the death of her husband, Mallie's father. He had the bad luck to fall off a pile of lumber at the lumber yard where he was working. He fell in front of an advancing forklift and was run over. He died later at the hospital of internal injuries. Even with the insurance money, it had been a struggle to make it sometimes. Dana was an office manager at a local real estate office. Bob Jenkins, the owner of the real estate firm, understood about Dana taking time off to be with Mallie. He always gave her time off when she asked for it. Mallie had helped out. She worked part time babysitting after school. Money had been tight at times, but they always made it, and Mallie was in her last year of nursing training. At twenty-two she was ready to start her life. She had to pull through. Dana could not stand the idea of going on without her daughter.

"Mallie, you have to hear me. I am not going to let you go. Hang on and come back to me." Dana gave Mallie's hand a squeeze and kept talking to her softly.

The door to Mallie's room eased open. Bob Jenkins peeped into the room. Dana looked up, startled.

"Bob," she exclaimed. "What are you doing here?"

Bob flushed slightly. He came forward and handed a large bouquet of flowers to Dana.

"I wanted to check and see how Mallie was doing," he responded.

"There has been no change," Dana sighed and looked at her boss. "It was very nice of you to come by. How are things going at the office?"

"Well," Bob looked down at Dana. He tried to hide the feelings he had for her, but he was sure they showed on his face. He had been trying to work up the courage to ask her out for a while. Bob was a rather shy person and he was afraid she would turn him down. Her whole world was tied up in her daughter, a daughter, who was now lying in a hospital bed on life support. They had no idea when or if she would wake up. "We are doing the best we can, but we miss you like crazy." He saw the look in her eyes at this statement and hurried to reassure her. "Don't worry, we will be fine. You take as much time as you need until Mallie gets better."

Dana smiled at him gratefully. "Thank you, Bob." She got up from the bedside and gave him a quick hug. She flushed slightly and hurried back to Mallie's bedside.

"Well," Bob stammered as he also flushed. "I'll see you later. Let me know how Mallie is doing."

"I will," agreed Dana. "Thank you for coming by and for the flowers."

"You're welcome. Take care." Bob turned and left the room.

Dana gazed after him thoughtfully. She had been attracted to him for a while, but she had no idea how he felt about her. She turned back to Mallie. She had no business thinking about Bob now. Mallie had to be her top priority.

Two doors down the hall was a young man, also in a coma. A twenty-six-year-old lawyer, only recently hired at a law firm, he had suffered an aneurysm and had collapsed three days earlier. His parents were taking turns staying at his bedside. Today was his mother's turn. She was talking softly to him, trying to get a response.

"Daniel Grey, you listen to me. It is not like you to just lie there. You are a fighter. Find your way back to us. I know you can do it. Don't give up. Come back to us, Son." Mary bowed her head as she prayed for her son's recovery.

The young man was walking down the beach. There was sand and water as far as the eye could see. He continued on, strolling slowly, enjoying the feel of sunshine on his face. In the distance he could see a girl sitting staring out across the water. She was just sitting there looking out at the water and didn't seem to be aware of his approach. He didn't want to startle her so he spoke while still some distance away from her.

"Hi," he called.

The girl looked his way, but she didn't look startled. She just stared at him and watched him approach.

"My name is Daniel Grey. I haven't seen you here before. I have been here for the last few days and the place has been deserted."

"I'm Mallie Wilson. This is the first time I have been here. It is a beautiful place, so quiet and peaceful." Mallie sighed and looked back out over the water.

"Do you want me to go?" Daniel asked, "I don't want to disturb you.".

"No, I am glad to have someone to talk to. It can get lonely sometimes." Mallie smiled at Daniel. He smiled back and took a seat beside her to gaze out over the water as they talked.

"Do you live around here?" asked Daniel.

"Yes," replied Mallie. "I live here in Denton. I am taking a nurses training course at the local college. I was on my way home from class when I was hit by a car. I am in a coma at the local hospital. I can hear my mother talking to me and it just breaks my heart when I can't respond to her. She sounds so sad." Mallie laid her head on her drawn up legs and fought to control her tears.

Daniel put an arm around Mallie's shoulder to comfort her.

"I know what you mean, I am in the hospital, too. I had an aneurysm while at work and I am in a coma, too. I have been in a coma for three days. I can hardly stand hearing my mom and dad begging me to wake up." Daniel sighed, heavily.

"Do they have you hooked up to a bunch of machines?" Mallie asked.

"Yeah, it almost drives me crazy listening to all those machines. The only thing worse would be if they turned them off. That is scary. I don't know what would happen then." Daniel shuddered as he imagined being without the help of the machines.

"Yeah, I know what you mean." Mallie rose to her feet. "I guess I need to get back and check on Mom. Do you want to walk back with me?" she asked.

"Sure," replied Daniel, rising to his feet. He took Mallie's hand and they continued to talk as they walked slowly back up the beach. Mallie told him about her father's accident and subsequent death.

"It must have been tough," Daniel replied. "I can't imagine being without either of my parents. They sometimes drive me crazy, but it is good to know they are there when I need them.

They must be going through torture now. Mom called my sister. She and her husband will be coming. She tried to reach my brother but he is in the Marines. All she could do was leave a message for him. I am glad my sister is going to be here for my mom. Dad tries, but he is just not an outgoing person. I know he feels things deeply, but he just doesn't seem able to express himself. I know my parents love each other. This is so hard on them."

"I don't have any brothers or sisters. It is just me and my Mom. My mom has been through a lot. It has been just the two of us for the last ten years since my dad died. She has always been there for me. I know my accident has to be awful for her." Mallie sighed heavily as she turned to Daniel. "Thanks for walking back with me. I had better go in now. Will I see you tomorrow?"

Daniel gazed into her face with a smile. "Yeah, I'll be here. It will be good to see a friendly face." He gave her hand a quick squeeze before releasing it. "Bye."

"Bye," Mallie replied as she disappeared.

Daniel disappeared also, returning to his body and the sound of the machines and his mother's prayers.

Mallie listened as her mother prayed for her recovery. She struggled to let her mother know she could hear her. She wanted to reassure her, but she could not make herself understood, she could not get through. It broke her heart that her mother had to suffer so.

Mallie was comforted to feel her mom's hand still holding onto hers. The machines were still going strong with all of their sounds. The door opened and the doctor came in.

"Hello, Mrs. Wilson. How are you doing?"

"I am alright. Can you tell me what's wrong with Mallie? Is she going to be alright?" Mrs. Wilson asked.

"Well," the doctor replied, "she has some swelling around her brain. We have to give it a few days and see if it goes away by itself. If it doesn't, we may have to operate. We can only wait and see."

"It could get better by itself?" Mrs. Wilson asked fearfully.

"Yes, it could." The doctor replied. "We just have to keep praying and hope for the best."

"Yes, thank you, Doctor."

Mallie was encouraged by what she heard. She could hardly wait until she could tell Daniel.

The doctor's next stop was two doors down. He entered Daniel's room with less cheer than he had entered Mallie's.

Daniel's mother looked up quickly at the sound of the door opening.

"Hello, Mrs. Grey." The doctor said as he came to the side of the bed.

"Hello" she replied. "Has there been any change?" She asked hopefully.

"I'm afraid not. The results of the tests are not all back yet. There seems to be very little brain activity. The tests indicate he may have suffered a stroke. We are not sure if there has been any permanent damage yet. We won't be able to run those tests until he wakes up."

"He will wake up, won't he?" Mrs. Grey interrupted the doctor with a question that she desperately wanted an answer to.

"We certainly hope so. We are doing all we can toward that goal. I'll be back to check on Daniel later."

The doctor abruptly turned and left the room.

"*What a jerk*," thought Daniel to himself as the doctor left. He tried to communicate with his mother, but he could not get her attention. He thought about Mallie. Instantly, he could hear her thoughts in his mind.

"*Hi, Daniel, are you in your room?*" Her thoughts were clear in his mind. It seemed as if they were together, face to face.

"*Yes, I am. How can I hear you so plainly?*" Daniel thought back to Mallie.

"*I don't know. I'm new at this. I just thought about you and there you were.*"

"*Can you hear me as plainly?*" Mallie loved the sound of Daniel's thoughts in her mind.

"*Yeah, it's like we are together. I love it. It has been so hard not being able to communicate with anyone.*"

"*I know. I haven't been out as long as you but it is scary. I am glad I am not alone anymore.*" Mallie continued to send her thoughts to Daniel. "*The doctor was just here. I don't like him very much. He doesn't seem to have any compassion for the patients or the people that are here for them. I am going to be much better at nursing than that. I have learned a lot, being a patient.*"

"*It sounds like we have the same doctor. I wanted to grab him and toss him out the door. He upset my mom and she doesn't need any more stress.*" Daniel sounded as if he could get up and give that doctor a piece of his mind.

Mallie laughed softly. Daniel grinned. He liked the sound of Mallie's laughter. It made him feel good inside.

Mallie listened as the nurse came in again and finally persuaded Dana to go to the cafeteria for something to eat. Dana resisted, but she finally decided that she needed nourishment. She reluctantly followed the nurse from the room, after one last look back at Mallie.

"How do you feel about a walk on the beach?" She asked Daniel. "My mom just went to the cafeteria for something to eat."

"I'll meet you there. My mom and dad are talking to each other. They will be occupied for a while."

In a flash both Daniel and Mallie were on the beach facing each other. Daniel grinned at Mallie as he reached for her hand. Mallie grinned back and they turned and began to walk up the beach. They walked slowly, talking softly to each other. They were just enjoying each other's company as they walked, holding hands, smiling at each other often, and getting to know each other. After a while they turned and started back.

"I'm glad that we got a chance to meet," Daniel smiled down at Mallie.

"Me, too," agreed Mallie. Giving Daniel's hand a quick squeeze. Mallie disappeared from view. Daniel grinned as he followed and was soon in his bed.

While Daniel and Mallie had been walking on the beach, Dana and Mary had been in the cafeteria getting some much-needed nourishment. Both ladies were too stressed to eat much, but both knew they had to eat. Their tables were next to each other, but they were both so deep in thought, they were not aware of anyone else. The nurse, who took care of both Mallie and Daniel, came into the cafeteria. She smiled to see both ladies there, eating. She walked over to their tables.

"Hello, Dana and Mary," she greeted both ladies. "I am glad to see both of you here. You needed to get out of those rooms for a while." She pointed to Dana, then Mary. "This is Dana Wilson and this is Mary Grey. You both have children in comas. Daniel is two doors down from Mallie. I hope I haven't over stepped, but I thought that you two might help each other."

The nurse quickly departed to get her own lunch.

"What happened to your son?" asked Dana.

"He had an aneurysm and collapsed at work. He is an attorney. What happened to your daughter?" asked Mary.

She was struck by a car. She was on her scooter on her way home from college. The boy in the car turned the corner and did not see her until it was too late. He is fine, but Mallie has swelling on her brain and is in a coma. We are waiting for the swelling to go down to see if she will need an operation. I'm sorry about your son. Is he going to be alright?"

"We don't know. All we can do is wait and see. It is very frustrating. I am sorry about your daughter, I hope she will be alright."

"Thank you. Do you live here in Denton?" Dana asked.

"Yes," replied Mary. "My husband owns the hardware store. We were very proud when Daniel decided to be an attorney. He was so happy when he passed the bar exam. I can't imagine what caused the aneurysm."

"Maybe the doctors will figure it out," replied Dana. "Mallie is in her last year of nursing training. She has worked so hard."

"What does your husband do?" asked Mary.

"My husband was killed ten years ago. He had an accident at the lumber yard where he worked. I work as an office manager at Bob Jenkins' real estate office."

"Oh," replied Mary. "You have had a rough time. I will keep Mallie in my prayers along with Daniel." She looked at the food left in front of her. "I don't think I can eat another bite. I think I'll get back to Daniel's room."

Dana looked at her own plate. "I don't think I can eat any more, either," she said. "I think I will head back upstairs."

The two ladies disposed of their trays and headed for the elevator. They were both anxious to see if anything had changed in their absence.

CHAPTER 2

$\mathcal{T}$he next day passed quietly. Dana and Mary met in the cafeteria again and shared a table. They talked more about their children and their lives in Denton. They found out they had a lot in common. It helped both of them to have someone, who understood what they were going through, to talk to.

Mallie and Daniel spent their time together on their private beach. They sat and talked about their dreams and hopes. Mallie leaned on Daniel and he sat with his arm around her. He was beginning to have very strong feelings for her, and she seemed to be getting closer to him. He hoped so. He couldn't stand to think the feelings were all one sided. Daniel rubbed his chin in Mallie's hair on top of her head.

"I guess we need to get back," he said.

"Yes," Mallie agreed. She took the hand he extended and allowed herself to be pulled to her feet. They walked back, slowly, holding hands, enjoying being together. When they stopped and turned to face each other, Daniel leaned forward *and gave Mallie a gentle kiss. Mallie felt her toes curl into the sand. She looked down in surprise.*

"I don't have any shoes on," she said in surprise. She looked at Daniel's feet. "You don't either."

Daniel looked down and grinned. "I guess we didn't think that we needed them," he said. "When I decided I wanted to go to the beach, I just thought about pants and a shirt, and suddenly I was wearing them." Daniel replied. I never thought about shoes until you mentioned them."

"I didn't either. I wonder if we are getting sand on our hospital sheets." Mallie laughed at the thought.

"I don't think so. I think that we are only here in spirit." Daniel said, sadly.

"Well," Mallie continued, gazing into Daniel's eyes. "However we got here, I'm just glad that I can be with you."

"Me, too," said Daniel, holding Mallie close for a few minutes. "We had better go in." Mallie disappeared and Daniel followed quickly.

Bob Jenkins entered Mallie's hospital room quietly. He knew he might not be welcome, but he just couldn't stay away.

Dana looked up as Bob entered. She had a surprised look on her face, but she didn't seem to be bothered that he had come to visit again.

"Hi, Bob." She rose and took Bob's hands as he extended them towards her. "It's good to see you," said Dana. I keep sitting here, waiting for some sign from Mallie. There has been nothing."

There were tears in her voice. Bob pulled her into his arms and held her close for a minute.

"Mallie is going to be alright. You have to give her time to heal. She is a strong girl and she is a fighter like her mom. With you in her corner, she will be better in no time."

Bob tightened his arm for a moment in reassurance and then released Dana and moved back slightly.

Dana wiped her eyes and sniffed back more tears. She smiled slightly at Bob.

"Thanks, I'm sorry for crying all over you. Sometimes it gets to be too much for me." She started to turn away but Bob held her arm gently.

"You can cry on me any time you need to. I will always be here for you and Mallie. You both mean a lot to me."

Dana smiled up into Bob's face as she studied him to see if he was sincere. He seemed sincere to her. She gave his hand a reassuring squeeze.

"Thank you, Bob." She was glad to see she wasn't the only one with feelings.

"Why don't you let me sit with Mallie while you go home, take a shower, and get into some clean clothes? I promise that if there is any change, I will call you back immediately." Bob told Dana. "You will feel much better able to cope with everything after a shower."

"Are you trying to tell me I smell bad?" Dana smiled at Bob.

"No," said Bob with an embarrassed look on his face. "I just thought you would feel better, and I know you don't want to leave Mallie."

Dana patted his arm. "I know. I was just teasing. If you are sure you don't mind, I could use a shower and a change of clothes. I can bring some clothes back with me for me and Mallie. There is no way she can wear what she had on at the time of the accident. They were destroyed. When she gets ready to come home, she will need something to wear."

Bob gave her hand a reassuring squeeze. "You run along. Don't worry about Mallie. I'll be right here."

Dana gave Bob a quick hug and hurried from the room after squeezing Mallie's hand and telling her she would be right back.

After Dana left, Bob settled into the chair at Mallie's bedside.

"I don't know if you can hear me Mallie, but I wanted to tell you that I am in love with your Mother. I have been for quite a while. I don't know if she feels the same. As soon as you are better, I'm going to ask her out. I want to see if there is any chance that we could make a future together. I know how close the two of you are and I would never try to change that. I just want to be a part of both of your lives. We are both pulling for you to get better." Bob reached for Mallie's hand and gave it a squeeze. He then settled back to wait for Dana's return.

Dana hurried into her small house. She quickly got a small overnight case and gathered a change of clothing for Mallie and herself. She put in a couple of gowns, a robe, and some slippers for Mallie. She included a brush and a few articles of makeup for Mallie to use when she woke up. After placing the case by the front door, she hurried to take her shower. Feeling much better, Dana decided to eat a sandwich before returning. Quickly, she put together a ham and cheese sandwich and a glass of milk. She made quick work of eating, rinsed the plate, and left it in the dish drainer. Dana grabbed the case, locked the door and headed back to the hospital. She had been gone less than an hour, but it felt much longer. She was anxious to get back to Mallie. It was sweet of Bob to help her take a break. She smiled. Maybe when this was over, and Mallie was all right, they could get together sometime.

"Hi, I'm back," said Dana as she entered Mallie's hospital room.

"That was quick," said Bob. "You look like you feel much better."

"I do. A shower and change of clothing were just what I needed. Thank you so much for staying while I was gone. Has there been any change?" Dana asked anxiously.

"No, everything is the same and I was glad to be able to help. Mallie and I had a nice little talk. Of course, I did the talking. She just listened," replied Bob.

Dana smiled. "I have been doing a lot of that. I don't know if she can hear me, but I want her to know someone is here for her. I don't know if it helps her but it helps me."

"You keep right on talking. No one knows how much a person in a coma hears." Bob gave her hands a reassuring squeeze. "I have to get back to work. If you need anything give me a call. I'll check back later, if that's alright."

"That's fine. Thank you so much for staying. You are welcome any time." Dana gave him a hug as he left.

Dana settled back into her chair at Mallie's bedside. She took Mallie's hand and looked at her closely. She had color in her face. It looked almost as if she had been out in the sun instead of being stuck in a hospital bed.

"Well, Mallie how would you feel about your mom going out with a real estate business owner? I really do think he likes me. Would you listen to me? I sound just like a teenager. I guess we never get too old to feel attracted to someone. If you were awake, I would never be talking like this. I am too old for this teenage nonsense. I do think he likes me though." She gave a soft giggle.

Mallie smiled softly to herself. She was glad her mother was about to crawl out of the shell she built around herself after the death of her husband. It was time for her to find some happiness. She thought about Daniel and smiled again. Maybe they were both ready for happiness.

~

Daniel and Mallie were on their beach again. Mallie was leaning back against Daniel and he had his arms around her. Mallie told Daniel about Bob and Dana and how she hoped they could get together. Daniel agreed. He thought it would be great for Mallie's mom.

"When this is over, will you go out with me?" he asked Mallie.

"I would like that," said Mallie, snuggling closer to Daniel.

"Ouch!" Mallie exclaimed, sitting up and looking at her arm.

"What's wrong?" Daniel asked.

"I don't know. I felt as if I were getting a shot." Mallie quickly got to her feet. "I had better go and see what's going on."

"Ok, I'll wait here for you,"

"Alright," Mallie answered.

She disappeared and was back in her hospital room listening to what was happening. The nurse was talking to Dana.

"Why are you giving her a shot?" asked Dana.

"We are going to take her down to x-ray and see if the swelling is going down. We want her relaxed while we do the scan." The nurse was busy preparing Mallie to be moved while she was talking. "We won't be long, about thirty to forty-five minutes. You can wait here if you want to."

"No," replied Dana. "I'm going down with you." She gave the nurse a determined look as if daring her to argue with her.

The nurse looked at her hard and then shrugged her shoulders. Let someone else deal with the patient's family, it wasn't her job. She rolled Mallie's bed out in the hall. An orderly was there to help take the patient down for tests.

Mallie flashed back to Daniel. She snuggled into his arms.

"They are taking me down for some tests. The nurse gave me a shot to relax me." Mallie yawned sleepily. I guess the shot is working," she said. She leaned into Daniel's arms almost falling asleep.

Daniel pulled her closer towards him and held her as she fell asleep in his arms. Mallie was asleep for almost an hour before she started to stir. She yawned widely. Daniel grinned at her.

"It's good to have you back," he said, holding her close. "I can tell you now that you don't snore," he teased.

"I could have told you that," she teased back. "Thanks for taking care of me."

"My pleasure," he replied.

"I had better go see what the tests show." Mallie gave his arm a squeeze and disappeared.

Daniel sat waiting for Mallie to return.

"I guess I need to see what's going on in my room," he thought. He disappeared and was soon in his bed.

CHAPTER 3

$\mathcal{M}$ary and Herman Grey were in Daniel's room. Herman had his arms around Mary in an awkward hug. He was trying to comfort her as she cried softly. They were not a demonstrative couple but he did the best he could to help her. His heart was heavy as he watched his youngest son lying so quietly.

"Katie and Brian will be here tomorrow." Herman said. Katie was their daughter and she was two years older than Daniel. Her husband, Brian, was some kind of computer whiz. Herman did not understand much about Brian's profession. He just knew Brian made a good living and he made Katie happy. Katie and Brian had a daughter, Sylvia. She was two years old and Brian's mother was looking after her. They did not want her waiting around at the hospital. Herman and Mary's older son, Matt, was serving in the Marines. They sent him a message, but there was no response as yet.

Mary pulled back as the door opened and the doctor came into the room. Mary and Herman both turned toward the doctor.

"Has there been any change?" Mary asked.

The doctor came to the bedside and looked at Daniel's chart. He then looked at him closely and felt his skin.

"I don't see any change, but his skin is warm to the touch and he has more color in his face. If I didn't know better, I would say he has been out in the sun."

The doctor put up the chart and turned to the anxious couple.

"We think the aneurysm was caused by a blood clot from his leg. It traveled up and blocked an artery. We are giving Daniel blood thinners to try and dissolve the clot. We will give the medicine a couple of days to work."

"What if it doesn't work?" Mary asked.

"Then we will have to operate and put in a stint to get the blood flowing again."

"Will he be able to wake up? Will he be alright?" Herman asked.

"We don't know. We have to wait and see how much damage was done by the clot. We won't be able to tell until he wakes up. I'll leave instructions for the nurse to start the blood thinner and I will check back tomorrow and see how he is doing."

The doctor left. Herman and Mary were speechless. They hardly knew what to think.

"I wish we could get another doctor. I don't like that doctor at all. He is too abrupt." Mary declared.

"At-a-girl-mom," thought Daniel. His mom was a great one for telling it the way it was.

"Let's give the blood thinner time to work. If it doesn't work, we might look into finding another doctor." Herman reassured Mary. She gave him a grateful smile and hugged him tightly. Herman hugged her back. He was glad to be able to make her feel a little better.

Daniel flashed back to the beach. He wanted to share the latest developments with Mallie.

Mallie had been listening to the conversation going on in her room. The obnoxious doctor was there filling Dana in on the results of her tests.

"Mrs. Wilson, Mallie's tests show the swelling has receded slightly. There is still quite a bit of swelling. It looks like a bone fragment may have been lodged in her brain. We will have to wait for the swelling to go down some more before we can be sure, but if it is a bone fragment we will have to operate. I will let you know as soon as I find out anything." After passing on the results of the tests, the doctor departed.

Dana wrung her hands together. She didn't know what to think. She pulled out her phone and called Bob Jenkins.

"Hello," Bob answered.

"Hello, Bob this is Dana. I didn't know who else to call. I just had some news about Mallie and I needed to talk to someone."

"I'll be right there." Bob hung up the phone and, grabbing his jacket, headed out the door.

Bob entered Mallie's room and quickly went to Dana. He put his arms around her and held her closely.

"Are you alright?" he asked.

"I don't know," said Dana. "The doctor said the swelling had gone down slightly. He then proceeded to tell me that Mallie may have a bone fragment in her brain. They can't be sure until the swelling goes down some more." She sighed. "I don't know where that doctor trained, but they sure didn't teach him anything about sensitivity."

"At least the swelling is getting better. We can be thankful for that." Bob was furious at the doctor for making things harder on Dana. "Do you know the doctor's name?"

"I really wasn't paying attention," said Dana. "I can ask the nurse next time she comes in."

"Do that," said Bob. "I would really like to know more about him."

"Ok," agreed Dana. She leaned closer to Bob. "I am so glad you are here. I needed to talk to a friend."

"I'll always be here for you, Dana." Bob looked down at Dana. "This might not be the time to tell you this, but I care for you and Mallie. When Mallie gets better I want to see more of you. Maybe we can go out for a meal sometime."

"I would like that," said Dana. "I would like that very much."

The nurse entered the room. She went to check on Mallie. She checked all of the machines and looked at the IV in Mallie's arm. She seemed to think everything was fine.

"Joyce," said Dana, after looking at the nurse's name tag. "Could you tell me what the doctor's name is? I forgot what he told me."

"He probably didn't tell you anything," sniffed the nurse. "His name is Drake, Marcus Drake."

"Thank you," replied Dana.

The nurse left and Dana turned to Bob.

"Well, you have his name. What are you going to do with it?"

"I'm not sure, yet," replied Bob. "Let me look into it."

"Ok, agreed Dana. "Thank you for coming so quickly. I was about to lose my cool."

"Now that is something I would like to see, the unflappable Mrs. Wilson losing her cool."

"Stop teasing," said Dana. "I'm serious."

"So am I," said Bob grinning down at her.

Dana smiled back at him. "You had better get back to the office. I'll call you if anything else happens. Thank you so much for coming."

"Alright, but you call if you need me."

"I will," promised Dana.

Dana went over and sat in the chair by Mallie's bed.

"He is one nice man, Mallie."

Mallie would have agreed with her, but she had left to find Daniel. Daniel was waiting for her on the beach. She went straight into his arms. They closed around her tightly. Mallie squeezed him back just as tightly.

"Are you alright, Mallie?" Daniel asked.

"Yeah, I'm ok. The doctor told my mom that I may have a bone fragment in my brain. They won't know for sure until the swelling goes down some more. If there is, they will have to operate."

Daniel tightened his arms around her again.

"He sounds like the same insensitive clod who was in my room. He told my parents my aneurysm was caused by a blood clot which had traveled up from my leg and was causing a blockage. He said they are going to give me some blood thinners and see if they work. If they don't, then I would have to be operated on to put a stint in. My mother really doesn't like the doctor's attitude."

Daniel grinned at the memory of his mother's response.

"Bob didn't like it either. He took the doctor's name. I don't know what he is going to do, but I hope it teaches the doctor that patients and their families have feelings."

Mallie snuggled back into Daniel's arms as they sat on the beach. They just sat quietly enjoying being together.

Daniel and Mallie stayed snuggled together most of the night. It didn't make any difference to them. It was always light where they were, unless they wanted it to be different. Daniel reluctantly sat up and prepared to go back.

"My sister and her husband are going to be here today and I need to be there. I wish you could be there to meet them, too."

Mallie patted him on the cheek. "I will meet them all later, after we wake up."

"Ok," agreed Daniel. With one last hug, he was gone.

Mallie sighed. It was lonely here without Daniel. She flashed back to her room. Her mom was asleep on the sofa bed that the nurse had fixed for her. Mallie looked at all of the machines she was hooked to. There was surely a lot of them. Sighing softly to herself, Mallie entered her body and settled into sleep.

Bob entered the real estate office early, but his assistant was already there. His assistant, Billy, was young but he was a whiz with the computer. There was nothing he couldn't do with it when he set his mind to it.

"Good morning, Billy." Bob said as he greeted him.

"Hi boss," replied Billy. "How is Mallie doing?" Mallie practically grew up around the real estate office. She was a favorite with everyone there.

"Mallie is about the same. The swelling has gone down a little, but she is still in a coma. The doctor seemed to think that she may have a bone fragment in her brain. He is waiting for the swelling to go down some more to be sure."

"Wow," said Billy. "The poor kid just can't catch a break."

"I know," said Bob. "I want you to find out all you can about Dr. Marcus Drake. He is Mallie's doctor. There is something about him that I just don't like."

"OK, I'll get right onto it boss." Billy turned to his computer ready to get to work.

Bob went into his private office to try and do some work. His mind was so full of Dana and Mallie, it was hard to concentrate.

Katie hurried into Daniel's room. After a fearful look at Daniel, lying so quietly in his hospital bed, she rushed into her mother's arms.

"Oh, Mom, has there been any change?" Katie looked back at Daniel. Brian followed her into the room. He quickly went and gave Mary a reassuring hug. He handed Mary a handkerchief as tears flooded her eyes.

"I don't know," responded Mary. "They are giving him blood thinners to try dissolving the clot. The doctor hasn't been by this morning. It may be too soon to tell if they are working."

"He has good color. He doesn't look as though he has been in this hospital bed for almost a week. Are the nurses keeping his legs and arms moving? They will get stiff, just lying there."

"Yes, they have a nurse come in once a day to give him a bath and massage his arms and legs." Mary replied. "He is very nice to us. He explains what he is doing and why. Not like that doctor. He can hardly take time to answer my questions."

"It sounds like you don't care much for the doctor," Brian

said. He smiled slightly at the thought of Mary tangling with the doctor.

Mary sighed. "I know the doctor is probably doing the best he can. It is just that his attitude needs adjustment. He should take a sensitivity class. People who are hurting don't need the extra stress."

Brian looked at his usually quiet mother-in-law in surprise. It was odd to hear her talk about feelings. She always seemed to have trouble expressing her feelings, except when it came to her children. Then she could be a regular tigress. That doctor must have really rubbed her the wrong way.

"Where's Dad?" asked Katie.

"He had to go to the store for a while. He had a shipment coming in. He wanted to check on it. He'll be back soon." Mary went over to the bed and took Daniel's hand and gave it a squeeze. "Would you like to go down to the cafeteria and get lunch before the rush starts?" Mary asked. "I can introduce you to Dana. She's two doors up from us. Her daughter is in a coma, also. She was in an accident. Dana and I have been meeting in the cafeteria. It helps to have someone to talk to, who understands."

"I would love to go down with you and meet Dana," said Katie. "Would you like Brian to stay with Daniel?"

"No, the nurse will be here in a few minutes to give him his bath and take care of him. Now is a good time to go."

The nurse entered as they turned to go.

"We are going to the cafeteria. Have me paged if there is any change," said Mary.

"I will," the nurse promised. "Have a nice lunch."

"Thank you," replied Mary as they left.

Meanwhile, Mallie's nurse arrived to give her a bath and massage her limbs. Dana gave her Mallie's gown and hair brush. She left instructions to call her in the cafeteria if there was any change before leaving to join Mary. The nurse smiled and assured her she would call. Then she ushered her from the room.

CHAPTER 4

Mallie and Daniel were back on their beach. They were sitting in their favorite position with Mallie leaning back in Daniel's arms. Daniel was holding her closely with his chin resting on top of her head. They were both comfortable and relaxed.

"When did you decide you wanted to be a nurse?" Daniel asked Mallie.

"When I was in high school there was a blood drive to help a young child with a bleeding disorder. I thought it was fascinating that my blood could help save a life. I started thinking about it and decided I wanted to do something in the medical field. Nursing was the easiest to enter. You don't have to go to school as long to be a nurse and you start earning money sooner. Besides, I like nursing." Mallie ended with a smile.

"You will make a great nurse," agreed Daniel. "I think you would be great at anything you set your mind to."

Mallie looked back at Daniel. "Thank you," she smiled.

"What about you," she asked. "Do you like being a lawyer?"

"I don't know," said Daniel thoughtfully. "I thought I

wanted to be a lawyer. I studied hard to be one and I made it, but I don't know if I can handle working in a large law firm. I don't have any say about which cases I handle. I don't like defending people I am pretty sure are guilty. Maybe I need to open my own office. That way I decide which cases to take and the ones to turn down."

"That's what you should do then," stated Mallie.

"Maybe," agreed Daniel. "The only problem is money. It would cost quite a bit to set up on my own. I don't know if I can do that now. I am going to have a lot of medical bills to pay off"

"Doesn't your law firm have insurance?"

"They have some but I don't know how much it will cover. I haven't been with them very long. I will have to wait and see."

Mallie snuggled closer to Daniel. She put her hands over his and held him closely. She sighed. She needed to go check on her mom but she hated to leave Daniel.

Mallie half turned toward Daniel and leaning back gave him a quick kiss.

"I have to check on my mom and see what the doctor is up to. I'll be back as soon as I can."

"Me, too." Daniel leaned forward and stole another kiss.

"Bye," said Mallie as she disappeared.

Daniel sighed. He hated being away from Mallie. He flashed to his own bed to see what was going on.

The nurse finished with Mallie's bath and massage. She combed her hair and dressed her in one of the gowns Dana gave her. She hung the robe on the back of the locker door and put the shoes in the bottom of the locker. The nurse rinsed the pan she had been using and left it in the bathroom. Dana came in as she exited the bathroom.

"Are you finished?" asked Dana.

"Yes, I am all done. Mallie looks nice in the gown you brought for her." The nurse smiled reassuringly.

"Yes, she does," agreed Dana.

"I'll see you later. If you need anything just push the call button." The nurse left as she gave these instructions.

Dana sat beside Mallie's bed and took her hand. "You look much better in your own clothes and out of that awful hospital gown. I'm glad I brought them from home." Dana talked to Mallie as she sat there. If there was any chance Mallie could hear her, she was going to keep trying to get through.

"I brought you some clothes to wear home, too. The ones you were wearing were in pretty bad shape. I think they will have to be thrown away if the police are finished with them. I don't know why they are bothering with them. I hope they are not hassling that boy. It was an accident pure and simple. The boy is so young. He must be scared to death. I know it is his fault you are lying here, but it was an accident." Dana sighed softly. It did no good to mess up that young person's life because of an accident. She would bet the young boy would be extra careful from now on. She just hoped Mallie didn't have to pay the price for his lesson.

Billy entered Bob's office with a hand full of papers.

"Here's the information you wanted about Mallie's doctor."

He handed the papers to Bob. Bob took the papers but looked impatiently at Billy.

"What do they say?" He asked.

"Well," said Billy, "he graduated third in his class at Harvard. He breezed through his resident and intern training. He doesn't seem to have many friends beside his roommate at

Harvard. His father is a big shot tycoon and his mother is high society. She spends all of her time at her club and doing charity work. Marcus was raised with a series of nannies. He didn't have much one on one contact with his parents except when they wanted to dress him up and show him off. Maybe that's why he doesn't show his feelings. He doesn't know how."

"Wow," said Bob. "There are no secrets from the internet. How did you find all of that so fast? Never mind." He held up his hand as Billy started to answer. "I wouldn't understand anyway. I'm just glad you're on my team."

Billy gave him a big smile. "I wouldn't be anywhere else, Boss. I like it here. What are you going to do about the doctor?"

"I don't know. I will have to think about it. Thanks."

"Sure thing, Boss," Billy said as he left the room to go back to work.

"Now that I have all of this information, what am I going to do with it? I guess I need to show it to Dana and see what she thinks." Bob grinned at the perfect excuse to pay Dana another visit.

"Have you heard anything from Matt?" Brian asked Mary.

"No, I left a message. So far, there has been no response."

"If you let me have the number, I may be able to find out something." Brian offered. Katie gave him a smile and squeezed his hand in thanks. Brian smiled back and returned the squeeze.

Mary went to her purse and found the number. "This is the only number I have. I will be glad for any help to get through. I don't know if he has received the message I left. Thanks for helping."

"I will try, but I can't promise anything," Brian replied.

"I know, but thanks for trying."

Brian took the number she offered and left the room. He went down to their rental car and opened his laptop. He soon had it up and running. His fingers flew over the keys as he looked for information on his brother-in-law. Brian's eyes widened at the information he was receiving. "Matt is doing alright," he murmured. He pulled out his cell phone and dialed the number Mary had given him. Glancing at the information from his laptop, Brian asked to speak to Matt's commanding officer.

"Hello, this is Major Davis. Who am I speaking to?"

"This is Brian Simms. I am calling about Matt Grey. He is in your charge and his brother is in a coma. His mother has been trying to get in touch with him but has had no luck. I was wondering if you could let him know what is happening."

"Just a minute," Major Davis pulled up some information on his computer. "I will get in touch with Captain Grey and he should be home by late tomorrow or early the next morning. I am sorry his mother had so much trouble getting a response. Please give her my best wishes for a speedy recovery for her son."

"Thank you. I will pass on your message."

Brian closed his laptop and, grinning widely, headed back to Daniel's room.

Katie took one look at Brian's face and ran to hug him.

"You got through," she said.

"Yes, Matt should be here late tomorrow or early the next morning. His commanding officer said he was sorry you had trouble getting a message to him. He also wished Daniel a speedy recovery." Brian told Mary.

Mary had tears running down her cheeks but a smile shone through. "Thank you so much, Brian." She came over and hugged him tightly.

"You're welcome," I am glad I could help," Brian returned her hug as he grinned at Katie over Mary's head.

"My husband, the genius," murmured Katie.

While Brian was arranging for Matt's homecoming, Bob was with Dana. He showed her the information that Billy had dug up on Dr. Marcus Drake.

"My goodness," said Dana. "Billy found all of this so fast. You had better hang on to him. He is a whiz kid."

"He is a whiz alright. I don't think he would like being called a kid though." Bob smiled at Dana.

"Sorry," said Dana. "I'll remember not to call him that. Thank him for me for the information."

"I will," promised Bob. "Although, I don't know what we can do with it. He is a very smart doctor. He just doesn't have any people skills."

"I'll have to think about it," said Dana. "At least, I can trust his judgment on Mallie's medical condition. The rest can be dealt with later."

Dana turned to Bob. "Thank you for reassuring me about Dr. Drake. I feel better about him now. He was so abrupt before, I wasn't sure I could trust his judgment." She gave Bob a hug, which he returned with enthusiasm.

"Daniel, are you there?" thought Mallie.

"Yes, I'm here. What's going on? Are you ok?"

"I'm fine. Bob just gave my mom a lot of information about our doctor. It seems he is very smart so we can trust his medical judgment. I guess he can't help being a jerk."

Daniel chuckled softly. "I love you," he declared.

"I love you, too. Want to go the beach?"

"Yes, definitely," responded Daniel.

In a flash, they were together, holding each other tightly, their lips sealed together.

"Wow, I never thought I would be in a coma when I fell in love," he held onto Mallie tightly.

"Me neither," Mallie snuggled under Daniel's chin, laughing softly. "I am so glad I found you. I can't imagine life without you."

"We are going to beat this and be together. It is meant to be. You are meant for me."

"And you are meant for me," responded Mallie.

They turned and, arms around each other's waists, started walking down the beach.

CHAPTER 5

"*Ouch,*" *Mallie exclaimed.*

"What's wrong?" asked Daniel.

"I think I just got another shot. They must be taking me down for another scan. I guess they want to check on the swelling. I suppose I will fall asleep again. We had better find a good place to sit."

Daniel led Mallie over to a place they used before to sit and relax. He sat down and pulled her down into his arms.

"Just relax," he told Mallie. "I've got you. Everything is going to be fine."

Mallie snuggled into his arms and in moments she was fast asleep.

Daniel sat holding her close, praying that everything would be alright.

Dana stuffed the papers from Bob into her purse. She did not want to take a chance on anyone else seeing them. It could cause bad feelings with the doctor if he found out.

Bob left saying he would be back soon. She was so distracted; she didn't think to ask where he was going. When the nurse came in to take Mallie down for another scan, Dana was ready to go with her. The nurse didn't try to stop her this time. She just shrugged and, after giving Mallie a shot, got her ready to go. The same orderly was waiting outside the room to help them get down to x-ray. The scan went smoothly. It only took about thirty minutes this time. They were soon in the hospital room again.

Dana could only sit and wait for the doctor to tell her the results of this last test.

~

On the beach, Mallie began to stir as the shot wore off. She looked up at Daniel and smiled. "This is getting to be a habit."

"I will always hold you when you need me," he promised.

Mallie looked at Daniel, seriously. "Will we have always, Daniel?" she asked.

Daniel tightened his arms around her. "Yes," he answered. "I won't have it any other way. I am not going to lose you now that I have found you. Some way we will be together." Mallie was reassured, but she was still worried. "I didn't get a chance to tell you before," said Daniel, "but my older brother, Matt, will be here tomorrow or the next day. Brian arranged it. He was able to get through to someone in charge and things went pretty fast after he talked to Matt's commander."

"I am so happy for your mother. I know it will make her feel better to see your brother," Mallie said.

"Yes," she was worried when she couldn't reach Matt. With

me in the hospital, she was really stressing out over everything else. She needed to have some control. Since she couldn't do anything about my condition, she had to find something else to control. Having Matt and Katie here will help." Daniel explained to Mallie.

"I know. I am so thankful my mom has Bob to distract her. I know she has feelings for him and he seems to have feelings for her. He has been a big help.. I hope they can get together when I wake up and everything gets back to normal," Mallie explained to Daniel earnestly.

"Things are never going to be normal again. At least not the normal of before because, when we wakeup, we are going to be together. We will have a new normal." Daniel held Mallie close.

"Yes, a new normal," sighed Mallie.

"Hello," said Bob as he stuck his head around Mallie's door. "Are you up for some Chinese food? I even have chopsticks or forks if you need them."

"I love Chinese food and chopsticks will be fine. Thank you. How did you know I like Chinese?" Dana came forward to help Bob with all the packages of food.

"I never forget anything about you," responded Bob. "You went out for Chinese food with Jane about a year ago. By the way, everyone at the office sends their best and they wanted to wish Mallie a speedy recovery."

"Thank them for me. They are a great group of people." Dana was teary-eyed at the thought of her co-workers' friendliness.

"Now, no tears,' said Bob gently. Mallie is going to be fine. Eat up."

Dana dug into the delicious smelling food. "Oh," she moaned "This is great. I am so glad you thought of it."

"Well, it's not how I pictured our first meal together, but I'll take what I can get. I'm just glad to be able to help a little." Bob gave Dana a big grin, which she returned after she swallowed a mouthful of Chinese food.

"You have helped more than a little. I would be lost without you. I am so thankful for your help and support, you have been a blessing for me." Dana gave a teary smile and went over to give Bob a hug. She hugged him tightly for a moment and then released him. "Thank you so much," she said again.

"I am glad I was able to help. You and Mallie are family to me. I will always be here for you. When Mallie gets better, I'm going to take you out for a big celebration." Bob assured Dana.

"I will look forward to it," agreed Dana.

"Good," said Bob. He and Dana started putting away the leftover food. When they had everything put away, Bob left to check in at his office. Dana smiled as she hugged herself. If Mallie would just wake up, everything would be perfect.

Dana had been waiting only a short while when the doctor came in to check on Mallie. He went over and checked her chart. He looked at her color and felt her skin.

"Is anything wrong?" asked Dana

"No, I was just surprised at how warm the patient is and she has very good color," he replied.

"Her name is Mallie," said Dana.

"What?" asked Dr. Drake.

"My daughter's name is Malinda or Mallie. She is not just 'the patient. " Dana explained.

"Yes, of course," Dr. Drake looked at her strangely, but didn't say anything.

"Has the swelling gone down any more?" asked Dana.

"Yes, it has. It still needs to go down further. It doesn't

look like the bone fragment is lodged in her brain. It looks as if it has moved down to the back of her head as the swelling has reduced. If it keeps coming down, it will be a very simple matter to remove it. We will have to keep a close watch on it. If she starts having seizures or spasms, let the nurse know at once." Dr Drake moved toward the door.

"Thank you, Dr. Drake," said Dana.

"Yes," he replied. He looked at Dana again strangely, before he left.

Dana smiled to herself. "You can catch more flies with honey than vinegar," she thought.

Dr Drake's next stop was Daniel's room. He entered and seemed startled at seeing so many people with the patient. Brian and Katie were there as were Mary and Herman. Dr. Drake went to Daniel's chart and checked it. He checked his color and felt of his skin.

"How is he doing?" asked Mary.

"He is doing better. His color is good and his skin is warm to the touch. According to his chart, his brain activity has increased. The blood thinner seems to be working," Dr. Drake delivered this news in a dispassionate tone. "We can continue the treatment for the time being." Dr. Drake nodded to everyone and headed out the door.

"Thank you, Dr Drake," called Mary as he left.

Dr. Drake merely waved his hand in her general direction as he went out the door.

Herman looked at Mary. "Why are you being so nice to the doctor?" he asked, curiously.

Mary smiled at her curious family. "Because Dana told me

you can catch more flies with honey than with vinegar," she replied with a grin.

Her family just stared at her with puzzled expressions on their faces. Mary laughed softly. Everyone relaxed. It was good to see Mary relax, no matter what the reason.

CHAPTER 6

The next evening, a military vehicle pulled up in front of the hospital. One soldier exited the vehicle then the driver drove around to find a parking place.

Brian was waiting in the lobby on the lookout for Matt. He smiled at this showing of prestige. "How are you, Captain?" he asked with a grin as he held out a hand to Matt.

"I'm doing good." responded Matt. He gave his own grin and pulled Brian into a hug.

"How's Daniel doing?" he asked.

"I think he's doing better. The blood thinner seems to be working, but he's still in a coma." Brian told him as they headed for the elevator to go up to Daniel's room.

"Look who's here," announced Brian as he preceded Matt into Daniel's room.

Everyone looked toward him expectantly.

"Oh, Matt!" exclaimed Mary. She hurried over to give her elder son a tight squeeze. Matt hugged her back and reached over to shake his father's hand.

"I'm sorry I couldn't get here sooner. Hi, Katie." He reached over to give his sister a hug.

"Well, look at you," exclaimed Katie. "Don't you look spiffy?"

Matt smiled. "My new rank came through a few days ago. I am a Captain now."

"That is great," exclaimed Katie.

"Oh, Matt, we are so proud and happy for you," Mary said.

"Yes, we are. You did good." Herman contributed. "How long will you be able to stay?" he asked.

"I have to check in with my commander, but I have a week before I have to return."

Matt turned toward Daniel's bed. It was strange to see his baby brother lying there, so still.

He walked over to the bed and took Daniel's hand.

"Hey, Little Bro, what are you doing, scaring us all this way? Don't you know you are supposed to be out chasing girls or adding to Mom's number of grandchildren. You can't take a powder on us, now. We need you around for a while yet. Come on back and put up a fight. You can do it. Find your way back to us, Daniel." Matt's eyes were moist as he gave Daniel's hand a last squeeze and left the bedside.

"What happened to him?" he asked the room in general.

"He had an aneurysm." replied Mary. "The doctor said the clot formed from a bruise on his leg. It traveled up and is causing a blockage. It caused him to have a stroke. The doctor is giving him a blood thinner to break up the clot. If it doesn't work, they will have to operate. They won't know if there is any other damage until he wakes up."

"Isn't there anything else they can try?" Matt looked as frustrated as they all felt.

"No, all we can do is wait." said Herman.

Matt looked around at everyone. "I have been traveling for

the last twelve hours. Would it be alright for me to go to the house, take a shower and grab a bite to eat?"

"Sure," Mary grabbed her purse and, taking out her key, handed the key to Matt. "Why don't you take a nap while you are there?' She gave Matt another hug. "I am so glad to see you," she said.

"I'm glad to see you, too, Mom," said Matt as he returned his mother's hug. Then giving them all a small wave he started out of the room.

"Do you need a ride?" asked Herman.

"No," he replied. "I have a car and driver waiting. He disappeared out of the door.

Brian chuckled at the looks on their faces. "He has a military vehicle and driver downstairs. I saw him when he drove up. The driver dropped him right in front of the door and left to park the car."

"Well, imagine that," said Mary.

Daniel chuckled to himself. His mom was impressed by his older brother. "Mallie," he thought.

"Hi, Daniel," Mallie answered in her thoughts.

"My brother was just here. My Mom was impressed because he had a car and driver waiting for him."

"That's nice," thought Mallie.

"Are you alright? You don't sound like yourself."

"I'm alright. I guess, I should be happy, the doctor told mom that the bone fragment is not in my brain. It has moved down. They will have to operate to get it out, but it won't be a serious operation. Do you think they will have to cut my hair? Mallie asked.

Daniel chuckled. "I don't know, but it will grow back and even with your hair cut, you will still be beautiful. I love you, Mallie. I like your hair, but I love you."

'Thank you, Daniel. I love you, too. Thank you for making me feel better."

"Would you like to take a walk?" asked Daniel.

"Could we just pop over to our place. I don't feel like walking, but I would like your arms around me."

"Let's go," said Daniel.

He was instantly on the beach and Mallie joined him. They sank down and Daniel enclosed Mallie in his arms.

"Now, I feel safe," Mallie sighed.

Matt's driver dropped him off at his parent's home.

"Come back for me in two hours," said Matt.

"Sure thing, Captain," replied the soldier giving Matt a salute, which he returned.

Matt turned and entered his childhood home. He stood just inside the door and looked around. There had been a few changes, but nothing significant. The hallway had been painted and he could see a fan turning in the living room to his left. He walked in, exploring to see what else was different from his last visit two years before. There was a new plant on the window sill in the kitchen. It was a large leafy plant and Matt smiled when he thought of his mother's green thumb. She could make anything grow. Matt continued on up the stairs and into his old bedroom. His mother had turned it into a sewing room, but it still had his single bed in it, so there was no reason for him to look for anywhere else to sleep. This would do fine while he was here.

Matt swung his duffle bag up onto the bed and removed the clothing from it. He hung his clothes on a hook on the back of the closet door. He just wanted to give the wrinkles a chance to fall out. He started to get undressed for his shower when he heard a call from downstairs. Going to the head of the stairs, he looked down into the hall.

"Can I help you?" he asked the young lady standing there.

The girl looked up at the sound of his voice. "Oh," she replied. "I'm sorry. I thought Mary or Herman would be here. I wanted to find out about Daniel's condition."

"There has been no change," replied Matt. "I am Daniel's brother Matt. Do I know you?" She looked familiar but Matt could not quite place her.

"Yes, you know me," she answered. "I live next door. I am Barbara Smith. I am the snotty little kid who used to drive you and Daniel crazy."

Matt grinned as he came down the stairs to where she stood. "Time has done quite a bit of improving," he declared.

"Watch it buster," said Barbara, grinning back at him. "I would say you have had your own improvements," she said giving a look over.

"Yes," agreed Matt. "I guess we both have been doing some growing up. How long has it been since we have seen each other?"

"Six years," replied Barbara. "I was away in college two years ago when you made a quick visit home."

"Oh." Matt looked at her enquiringly. "What did you study in college?"

"Cooking," said Barbara proudly. "I own a bake shop down-town. I make the best donuts around here."

"That's great," said Matt. "I will have to make it by there while I am here."

"How long are you staying?" Barbara asked.

"A week," said Matt. "I hope that Daniel will get better before I have to go."

"I hope so, too. I have been getting updates from Mary and Herman. Katie even stopped by the bake shop for a few minutes. She really came in to get some donuts, but it was good to see her. We used to be good friends. She was the sister I had always wanted. When we got together, we caused all kinds of mischief. She helped me pull a few of the tricks that I played on you and Daniel. I was happy for her when she and Brian got together, but I was sorry they moved so far away. I hardly ever get to see her now. Your Mom keeps me up to date on what is happening with all of you. When Katie came by the bakery, she showed me some pictures of her little girl. She is adorable."

"Yes, she is," Matt agreed. "Mom has also kept me up to date with pictures of her first grandchild."

"Well," said Barbara. "I had better go and let you get back to what you were doing. It was good seeing you. Don't forget to stop by for some donuts."

"It was nice to see you, too. I hope I'll see more of you while I'm here."

Barbara turned and flashed him a grin as she left. Matt felt his breath catch as he went back upstairs to get his delayed shower.

Mallie stirred where she lay wrapped in Daniel's arms. Daniel was leaning back against a boulder and they had both been sleeping. Daniel woke when he felt Mallie stirring.

"Where did this come from?" she asked, indicating the boulder.

"I wished for something to lean against and it appeared." Daniel grinned at Mallie. "It's convenient having what you wish for."

"Well," said Mallie. "I wished for both of us to get well, but so far it hasn't happened."

"I know, but it will. You and I are going to have a long life together." Daniel hugged her closely.

"We need to get back and see what's going on. Let me know as soon as you find out anything," he told Mallie.

"I will. You let me know what the doctor has planned for you. I want to be right there with you whatever happens."

"Ok," agreed Daniel.

After another hug and kiss they flashed back into their bodies.

Dana was still sleeping, but she stirred when Mallie returned. It was almost as if she felt Mallie's presence. She settled back into sleep. Mallie fell asleep, too. Even though she and Daniel had been sleeping, she was still tired. Maybe it had something to do with the coma.

"Goodnight, Love," she thought to Daniel.

"Goodnight, My Love," responded Daniel in his thoughts.

Mallie smiled to herself. She was so happy to have Daniel in her life.

The nurse came by early. Dana had just awakened. She started preparing Mallie for another scan.

"Isn't it a little soon for another scan?" asked Dana.

"Dr. Drake wanted to check on the bone fragment. He wants to get it out as soon as possible." The nurse never paused in what she was doing.

Dana looked on with a frown. She hoped that when Mallie became a nurse she would have a better attitude. The people at this hospital, at least most of them, could use an attitude adjustment. Some of them were so abrupt.

"Daniel," thought Mallie. "They are going to take me down for another scan."

"You just had one. Never mind. Meet me on the beach. We know you will be sleeping for about an hour."

"Ok."

Daniel and Mallie both appeared instantly at their place on the beach. Daniel put his arms around her and they sank together onto the sand into a good resting place. Daniel leaned back against the boulder and pulled Mallie closer into his arms. Mallie snuggled into him and was almost instantly asleep.

About forty-five minutes later, Mallie started to stir.

Daniel frowned as he looked down at Mallie.

"Does it seem to you the medicine they give you before the scan, is wearing off quicker?" Daniel asked Mallie.

Mallie scrunched up her nose thoughtfully.

"Yes, it does." I wonder what that means. Do you suppose I am building a tolerance to the medicine? That can't be good." Mallie frowned. "I don't know what I can do about it. I have no way of letting them know. They should be monitoring me, but I don't think they are." She sighed. "Maybe it will be over soon. If the bone is in the right place, the doctor will take it out. I shouldn't be having all of these scans then."

Daniel gave her another reassuring squeeze. "Let's go see what the scan shows."

He and Mallie were instantly in their rooms.

Dana was on the phone with Bob.

"The nurse took her down for another scan," Dana answered an unheard question. "I just have to wait for the doctor to tell me what the results are. No, you don't need to come over right now. I'm just sitting here waiting for the results. I know your business needs you. I'll call when I hear anything. Bye."

Dana hung up the phone. She wandered over to Mallie's bedside. "Oh, Mallie, please be alright. I can't stand the thought of losing you. Please come back to me." Dana held Mallie's hand as she begged her to get better. Please, Mallie," she said, crying softly.

Katie had talked Mary into going home for a shower and food, and maybe a nap. Brian was staying with Daniel. Herman was expected soon and Matt would be coming back. It was the perfect time for Mary to take a break. Brian talked to Daniel as if he could hear all that was being said. He told him about his niece and the things she had been up to. She was a very energetic child and kept Katie and Brian on their toes, but they loved her dearly which sounded through loud and clear as Brian spoke.

Daniel chuckled to himself.

"What's funny?" inquired Mallie.

"I was just listening to Brian talking about his and Katie's little girl. She sounds great. I can hardly wait until we have one of our own."

"Now wait a minute!" exclaimed Mallie. "There a few processes we have to get through before we can plan on a child."

"I know," soothed Daniel with a chuckle. "I was just dreaming."

Mallie smiled. "It is a nice dream. I love you Daniel."

"I love you, too. Now we just have to get well so we can get started on our little girl."

"Oh Daniel," laughed Mallie. "What's that noise I hear?"

"That's my brother Matt. He just came in and he and Brian are talking."

"Oh, I'll talk to you later enjoy your brother's visit." Mallie pulled back and tuned her senses into her room.

CHAPTER 7

he door to Mallie's room opened and Dr. Drake entered. He came over and checked Mallie's chart. He looked at her color before turning to Dana.

"How is she? Has the swelling gone down more?" asked Dana.

"Yes, the swelling has reduced some more, but it still has more healing to do. The bone fragment has moved down so that it is just below the skull cap. We need to go in tomorrow morning and remove it before it moves into a place that is harder to get to. We also want to prevent it from doing any additional damage. The nurse will bring you the necessary papers for you to sign and prepare Mallie for surgery. Mallie will be the first patient in the operating room in the morning."

"Will the operation take long?" asked Dana.

"It will take from forty-five minutes to an hour." With this bit of news, the doctor left.

Dana picked up her phone to call Bob. She then noticed the time. It was only another hour until the work day ended.

She would give Bob time to see his workers off before she called.

~

"Daniel," thought Mallie.

"I'm here," Daniel thought back.

"The doctor was just here. They have me scheduled for surgery in the morning. They are going to remove the bone fragment."

"I'll meet you on the beach."

Daniel and Mallie were instantly on the beach. Daniel enclosed Mallie in his arms.

He drew back slightly and looked at Mallie. "What did the doctor say?" he asked.

"He said the bone fragment is just below the skull cap and they want to get it out before it moves into a worse spot or causes any damage. It makes sense, but I am so scared."

Mallie snuggled closer to Daniel. He held her tightly, trying to soothe her fears. That was hard to do, considering he was just as scared.

While Daniel tried to reassure Mallie, Brian and Matt were talking in Daniel's room.

"Where are you going to be stationed when you go back, or can't you tell me?" pried Brian.

"I have a month left overseas, then I will be back in the states. I'm not sure where I will be, yet. I hope I will be close enough to home to be able to visit more. I have missed seeing everyone. Letters don't fill the need to see my family." Matt looked sad.

"I know what you mean. I don't think I could handle being

away from Katie and Sylvia. It's hard just leaving Sylvia with mom while we are here. Katie has already called a dozen times to check on her." Brian smiled ruefully at the thought.

"Being married and a mother really agrees with Katie. I don't think I have ever seen her so happy." Matt smiled at Brian.

Herman stuck his head inside the door. "Where's Mary?" He asked.

"Katie took her home to shower and rest." responded Brian.

"I convinced her that, between the three of us, we could keep an eye on Daniel." Brian chuckled. "I think the real reason she went was so that she and Katie could call and talk to Sylvia. It's been a couple of hours since Katie called my mom. I know she was itching to get out of here and call."

Herman smiled. "You and Katie will have to come back for a visit when Daniel is better and bring Sylvia."

"We will," agreed Brian.

"By the way, Dad, A girl named Barbara stopped by the house while I was there. She wanted to know how Daniel was doing. She claims to be the same skinny little thing with freckles who used to pester us with Katie. Is she Daniel's girl-friend?" Matt waited for Herman's answer.

"No, she and her folks are just friends of the family. They have lived next door for years, so she comes over every now and again to visit. She owns the bake shop in town. She makes great donuts."

"She sure does," agreed Brian. "Katie went there and brought some back. I think she wanted to see Barbara, she said they were like sisters when they were growing up. The donuts from the bake shop melt in your mouth. I don't think I have ever had any as good before. Katie and I will have to stop before we leave and get some to take home with us." Brian sighed, just thinking about eating more of the sweet treat.

I was just telling Brian that my tour overseas will be up in about a month, then I will be back in the States. I am hoping I will be close enough to visit more often.

Herman's face lit up at this news. "That would be great," he said. It will make your mom so happy. She misses all of you when you are not around."

"I miss her and you, too," replied Matt.

Herman flushed at this display of affection, but he looked pleased at Matt's words.

Bob came into Mallie's room to see Dana staring out the window, looking depressed. He went over and put an arm around her. "What's wrong?" he asked.

"The doctor has Mallie's surgery scheduled for in the morning. They are going to remove the bone fragment."

Dana leaned into Bob, loving the feel of his comforting arms around her.

"Why didn't you call me?" demanded Bob.

"He just told me a little over an hour ago. I knew you would be here as soon as the office closed. Besides, there was nothing you could do. We just have to wait for morning."

Bob was happy at Dana's words. She was coming to trust in his feelings and to depend on him. It made him happy to know Dana knew he would be there as soon as the office closed. Now, if Mallie would just get better, he could work on his and Dana's relationship. There was no way he was going to let anything stop what they were building. When Mallie woke up, he fully intended to make a life for the three of them.

Bob led Dana over to the sofa. They sat and he enclosed her in his arms as they settled back to wait for morning.

"You don't have to stay," sighed Dana.

"I'm not going anywhere. Just relax," soothed Bob.

～

It was a long night for Daniel and Mallie. Daniel knew the only thing he could do was hold her closely and let her know he was there for her. The only way they knew it was morning was when Mallie felt the prick of a needle and knew they were preparing her for surgery. She felt them pull her hair up, pin it, and then shave the bottom of her scalp. She hugged Daniel tighter as she felt them working with her hair. She knew she would be falling asleep, soon. She could only hope she would be waking when it was over.

～

"*They are shaving the back of my scalp,*" *she told Daniel.*

"*It will grow back.*" *said Daniel.* "*Don't worry, you will always be beautiful. Relax, I will be right here. I won't leave for a minute. I will still be holding you when you wake up. I love you,*" *he whispered.*

"*I love you, too,*" *whispered Mallie, groggily.*

Daniel sighed as Mallie fell asleep in his arms. He leaned back against the boulder and pulled her closer. It was going to be a long couple of hours.

～

The doctor came into the surgery waiting room where Bob and Dana were waiting. They had been waiting for almost two hours since they took Mallie downstairs.

Dana rose from her seat at once when she saw the doctor.

"Is it over? Is Mallie alright?"

"The operation went well. We got the fragment out with no complications. Mallie will be in recovery for about twenty minutes and then she will be taken back to her room. Why don't you go to the cafeteria and get some breakfast and then meet the nurse in Mallie's room? You can't do anything for Mallie while the anesthesia wears off and you will be better able to cope with some food." Dr. Drake encouraged Dana.

"Thank you, Dr. Drake. I think I could use something." Dana smiled at the doctor and squeezed Bob's hand.

They headed toward the cafeteria as soon as the doctor left.

"You know," said Dana thoughtfully. "Dr. Drake sounded almost thoughtful there for a moment. Maybe we are starting to get through to him."

Bob chuckled. "With you and Mary working on him he doesn't stand a chance. He may as well surrender and be done with it."

"Well," said Dana. "It will be to his benefit as well as his patients to humanize him."

Bob chuckled again as they made their way into the cafeteria.

"Oh," said Dana. "There's Brian. Let's see how Daniel is doing."

They headed over to the table where Brian and Matt were sitting, drinking coffee.

"Hello, Brian," said Dana. "How's Daniel doing this morning?"

"Hello, Dana. There's been no change. This is Daniel's brother Matt." He indicated Matt at the table with him. "Matt this is Dana. Her daughter is in a coma, too."

Both Matt and Dana said "Hello."

"This is Bob Jenkins," said Dana, indicating Bob.

The guys all shook hands and said "Hello, nice to meet you."

"Why don't you join us?" said Brian. "How is Mallie doing?"

"She had surgery this morning to remove the bone fragment. She is in recovery now and the doctor said that she was doing good." Dana filled them in on the latest developments.

"I'm glad she's alright," responded Brian. "Let us know if there is anything we can do to help."

"I will. Thank you," said Dana.

"We have to get back upstairs. Enjoy your breakfast. I hope everything goes alright for Mallie." Brian and Matt rose from their chairs and prepared to leave.

"Thank you," said Dana.

"They are nice people," said Dana, after they left.

"Yes," agreed Bob.

Matt and Brian paused outside of the cafeteria.

"I think I will head back to the house for a while," said Matt.

"Ok," said Brian. "Do you need a key?"

"No, I stopped at Dad's store and had a copy made yesterday. I didn't want to have to keep taking Mom's key."

"I'll let the folks know where you have gone. Get a little rest," encouraged Brian.

"I will," responded Matt. "Thanks."

Matt called his driver to meet him out front and walked towards the front door.

Brian chuckled as he made his way back to Daniel's room. It was something seeing his brother-in-law call for a driver whenever he needed a car.

"Where's Matt?" asked Mary, looking around Brian when he came in alone.

"He headed back to the house to freshen up. I think he just wanted some fresh air." Brian gave his opinion to the room at large.

"Did he say when he will be back?" asked Mary.

"He said two or three hours."

"He'll be back, don't worry," Brian gave his mother-in-law a quick hug for reassurance.

Matt didn't head straight home when he left. He had the driver go through town and stop at the bakery. He told the driver to wait and went into the shop.

The bell over the door rang as he walked in.

"Be right with you said a familiar voice from the back room."

Barbara emerged from the back room. She was wearing an apron, a covering on her head, and there was a dusting of flour on her face. She was beautiful.

Barbara grinned when she saw Matt.

"Hi," she said. "Come to sample my donuts?" She looked at Matt, teasingly.

"Yes," agreed Matt, "and to ask you to have dinner with me tonight."

Barbara looked thoughtful. "It would have to be local. We wouldn't have time to go anywhere else. I don't close the shop until eight."

"Where do you suggest? It's been a while since I dined in any of the places around here. Is Marshel's still open?"

"Yes, Marshel's will be fine," agreed Barbara. "I'll meet you at the hospital about eight thirty."

"Ok," Matt nodded. "Now about these famous donuts, I'll take four dozen. Mix them up."

Barbara looked at him in surprise. "You must have some sweet tooth." She remarked.

Matt chuckled. "I intend to pass them around. I want a

dozen to give another lady at the hospital. Her daughter is in a coma, too. I thought they might cheer her up a little."

"That's nice of you," Barbara looked at Matt approvingly.

Matt flushed slightly at the praise. He had not been trying to score points with Barbara when he thought about taking Dana some donuts, but, he was glad she liked the idea.

"I'll see you tonight," he said as he turned to go.

When Matt got to the car, he placed the donuts on the back seat and instructed his driver, Corporal James, to take him home. At the house, he retrieved the boxes from the back seat and handed one to the driver.

"You can pass these out to your buddies," He told the surprised Corporal James.

"Thanks, Captain." Corporal James said. "They will be surprised. What time do you want me to pick you up?"

"It'll be a couple of hours. I'll call you," responded Matt. With an exchange of salutes, Matt turned to go inside.

Mallie started stirring and Daniel tightened his arms slightly.

"Are you alright?" he inquired. He had been sitting there, holding her and worrying about the operation. He figured as long as she was there in his arms, she was alright.

"I think so," said Mallie. She yawned and smiled at Daniel. "I guess the anesthesia is still wearing off."

"I have been so scared," admitted Daniel.

"I know. Me, too." Mallie rested against Daniel. She was just glad the operation was over. "I guess I need to go and see what is going on in my room, but I don't want to leave you."

"I need to check in at my room, too, but it is so nice just to stay here and hold you in my arms."

Daniel held her a little longer before loosening his hold. "I guess we had better go. Let me know what is happening."

"I will. You are always just a thought away." Mallie squeezed his arm and disappeared.

Daniel sighed and did his own disappearing act.

Bob and Dana were sitting quietly on the sofa. He had his arm around her and they were talking softly. They must have been trying not to disturb her, Mallie thought.

Mallie settled down on the bed as she entered her body. Her head felt strange where the nurse had shaved the back of her head. They had her lying on her stomach with her head turned to the side, so the place on her head, where she had been operated on, was not disturbed. It was not very comfortable, but at least she was not in a lot of pain. The shots she had been given before and after the operation must be keeping the pain away for now, she reasoned.

Mallie tuned into what Bob and Dana were saying.

"I am glad the bone fragment is gone. I just wish the swelling would disappear and Mallie would wake up." Dana sniffed into the handkerchief that she was twisting in her hand. It must have been Bob's handkerchief. Mallie knew her mom did not carry handkerchiefs around with her.

"I know," Bob gave her shoulder a reassuring squeeze. "It won't be long, according to the doctor. We just have to be patient."

"I'm trying, but it is so hard to keep on waiting." Dana turned her face into Bob's chest and gave way to more tears.

Bob held her closely and let her cry. He thought the crying may help her release some of the tension and help Dana to feel better.

With a last sniff, Dana sat up straighter but did not move out of Bob's arms. "I'm sorry," she said. "I don't know what's come over me. I keep crying all over you."

"I am glad to be here for you. Don't worry about a few tears. It's a good outlet for stress. Don't you feel better, now?"

"Yes, I do." Dana sounded surprised.

"Good." Bob smiled at her.

"Daniel," Mallie thought.

"I'm here," thought Daniel back.

"The operation was a success. They just have to wait for the swelling to finish going down. Mom is really stressed out. Bob is trying to comfort her and I think it is working. Those two are really getting close."

"How do you feel about the two of them getting together," asked Daniel.

"I think it is great," said Mallie. "After all, you and I are going to be together when we wake up. So, I'm glad Mom won't be alone."

"I can't wait," said Daniel.

"Me neither," replied Mallie.

Matt was sitting in a chair, in Daniel's room, talking to his parents. Brian and Katie had gone back to the house to get a rest and check on Sylvia. The door opened and Barbara entered. Matt stood up.

"Hello, Barbara," Mary quickly rose and went to give Barbara a hug.

"Hi, how is Daniel doing?" Barbara asked.

"There hasn't been any change," said Mary.

"I'm sorry," said Barbara. "At least he hasn't got any worse. Maybe he'll start to get better soon."

"Are you ready to go?" He asked her.

"Yes," she answered.

"Where are you going?" asked Mary, puzzled.

"Barbara and I are going out to dinner." Matt responded. Barbara flushed slightly.

"Oh," said Mary. Her face brightened as she thought about this. "Well, have a good time."

Herman chuckled as they left. "He certainly doesn't let any grass grow under his feet."

"I'm glad he's getting out and having a good time. Barbara is a good girl. I think she has always had a crush on Matt. When she was a teenager, she was always hanging around where she could bump into him. Matt didn't have a clue about her feelings. He just treated her like he treated Katie. I think that's about to change." Mary laughed at the thought.

Herman just chuckled, again.

CHAPTER 8

att took Barbara's arm as he guided her into Marshel's. A greeter was standing at the door. Matt gave his name and the greeter took them to a table.

"Will this be all right?"

"Yes, this is fine." agreed Matt.

He held Barbara's chair for her before the greeter could. The young man seemed surprised by Matt beating him to the chair.

"Here are your menus. I'll be right back for your orders." The young man departed, leaving Matt and Barbara time to study the menu.

"What looks good?" asked Matt.

"I think I'll get a salad," said Barbara.

Matt gave her a surprised look. "You're not a vegetarian, are you?"

"No, but did you see how expensive everything is on this menu?"

Matt grinned at her. "Don't worry about it. I can afford it. Get what you like." When she still didn't look like she was going to order anything, Matt decided to take things into his own hands.

"Do you like seafood?" he asked.

"Yes," said Barbara.

"How about if we get a seafood platter and share it." Matt suggested.

"Ok," said Barbara.

The waiter came over with their glasses of water and utensils. "Are you ready to order?" He asked.

"Yes, we would like a seafood platter, two side salads and a large slice of chocolate cake."

"What about drinks?" he asked.

"Is a soft drink ok with you?" Matt asked Barbara. When she nodded, he ordered two soft drinks.

The waiter took their menus and left to put in their orders.

Matt looked over at Barbara. "What got you interested in donuts?" he asked.

"I have always been interested in baking." answered Barbara. "When I was little, I would help my mom with the baking. I loved it. I hit a rebellious phase during my teens when you couldn't get me in the kitchen for anything. That was when I used to follow you and Daniel around. I got over that and went back to my first love, baking. What about you, why did you join the Marines?" she countered.

Matt thought for a minute. "I guess, I just wanted to travel and see other places. After taking JROTC in high school, the Marines was the route I chose to follow my dream of seeing the world."

"Is it exciting?" asked Barbara.

"It can be, but sometimes it can be lonesome. You get close with your fellow officers, but you miss your family. That's why I'm glad to be coming back to the States. I want to be able to check in with my family on a regular basis."

"How much longer will you be in the Marines?"

"I have two more years. I don't know about after my time is up. They will probably try to get me to sign up for another tour. I don't know if that's what I want. I don't know what I would do if I got out. I'm going to have to think about it."

They paused in their conversation while the waiter brought their food and set everything up on the table.

"If you need anything else, just let me know," he instructed.

"Thank you," replied Matt.

"This looks good," said Barbara.

"Dig in," Matt said as he started filling his plate.

Barbara put some of the seafood on her plate and took a bite. "Oh," she moaned. "This is so good." They didn't talk for a while as they dug in and enjoyed their food. Finally, Barbara leaned back. "I can't eat another bite. I'm stuffed."

"Oh, no, you're going to help me eat the chocolate cake. Here it comes, now." Matt turned toward the waiter as he sat a large slice of chocolate cake on their table. "Come on take a bite." Matt took a forkful of cake and held it to her lips until she opened her mouth, then gently pushed the cake inside.

"Ooooh," moaned Barbara. She took a fork filled serving of cake and held it up to Matt's lips. He obediently opened and slowly savored the cake. They took turns feeding each other until the cake was gone.

"That was great," said Barbara. "I don't know if I can move, I'm so full, but I enjoyed every bite."

"So did I," agreed Matt, "Especially the company. Are you ready to go?" He pulled out her chair and, leaving a generous tip for the waiter, guided her out of the restaurant. Corporal James was waiting for them at the door. Matt helped Barbara into the back seat and climbed in with her.

"Do you want to go home, Sir?" asked Corporal James.

"Yes, the young lady lives next door to my parents."

Corporal James drove off and arrived at his house in no time. "Thank you," Matt told Corporal James when they got out of the car. "I'll see you in the morning at Oh six hundred."

"Yes, Sir." The soldier saluted and, when Matt returned the salute, drove

off.

"I'll walk you next door," said Matt taking her arm.

Barbara didn't say anything until they stopped in front of her door. "I had a great time and the food was fabulous,' she said.

Matt remained silent. He just smiled and drew her into his arms. As his lips touched hers, both felt the tingle all the way down to their toes. Matt deepened the kiss. When he finally pulled back, they were both breathing hard.

"Wow," said Barbara.

"Yeah, wow," Matt agreed.

"Can you meet me for lunch tomorrow?" asked Matt. It'll have to be quick. I have to be at the hospital as much as possible."

"How about we meet in the hospital cafeteria." suggested Barbara.

"Ok," agreed Matt. Just call me when you are ready and I'll meet you there."

"Alright, good night," she said.

"Good night," said Matt. After a quick brush of the lips, they parted to go to their respective homes.

First thing the next morning the doctor came by and checked on Daniel. Matt and Herman were there with him. Mary had gone home for a while when Herman arrived. Katie and Brian hadn't come in, yet.

"How's he doing?" asked Matt. The doctor looked over at the man in uniform as if he had just noticed him. Matt came forward and offered his hand. "I'm Daniel's brother, Matt." He explained.

The doctor shook his hand before explaining Daniel's condition. "He seems to be doing better. We are taking him down to x-ray this morning. I want to be sure the clot has dissolved. I'll have to evaluate his condition after we run some tests." The doctor started to leave after giving this news.

"Thanks, Doc," said Matt. The doctor nodded briefly and continued on his way.

Herman chuckled when he saw the look on Matt's face at the doctor's abrupt attitude. "Your mother has been trying to teach him some people skills. He is much better than he was when we brought Daniel to the hospital. Your mother and Dana decided to help him loosen up around patients and their families. I think they are enjoying themselves. It gives them something else to think about for a while and I can't see it doing any harm. It might help." He ended with a sigh.

Matt chuckled. He sounded just like his Dad, he thought. "If anyone can help him, Mom can."

The door opened and Katie and Brian entered. They were followed by the nurse who came to take Daniel down to x-ray.

"What's going on?" Katie querried.

"They are taking Daniel down to x-ray," responded Herman. "They want to check on the blood clot."

He stood to one side of the door and held it open for the nurse.

"Mallie," thought Daniel.

"I'm here," said Mallie.

"They are taking me down to x-ray."

"Did they give you a shot?"

"Not so far. I don't know what they are going to do when we get downstairs."

"Do you want to meet on the beach?" Mallie waited for his answer.

"Not yet, I want to see what they are doing, or hear what they are saying. If they give me a shot, I'll meet you."

"Ok," agreed Mallie. "Keep me posted."

"I will," agreed Daniel.

They wheeled Daniel into x-ray. The nurse turned him over to the technician.

"What do we have here?" questioned the technician.

"The doctor ordered an x-ray of his chest and his leg. He wants to see if a clot had dissolved and what had caused it. He wants to be sure there will be no future clots to cause problems. He also ordered blood work."

"You have to take him across the hall for the blood work." The technician informed her.

"I know," she said. "I was just thinking out loud."

While the technician wheeled Daniel into the x-ray machine and got him set up, he turned a smile on the nurse. "When are you going to break down and come out with me?" he inquired.

"Now, why would I want to do that?" asked the nurse. "You are nothing but a flirt. You have already gone out with over half of the nursing staff."

"I can't help it if I'm irresistible to the ladies." He grinned.

"Well, here's one that can resist you." She declared with a sniff.

He just smiled back at her. "You know you would have a good time."

The nurse just sniffed again and turned to wait for Daniel. The technician smiled and got on with his job. The nurse was soon wheeling Daniel across the hall for his blood work. That was taken care of quickly and they were on their way back to Daniel's room. She wheeled Daniel into his room where his anxious family was waiting for him. They knew it would do no good to question the nurse. They would have to wait for the results from the doctor.

"Thank you," Mary smiled at the nurse.

The nurse just smiled an acknowledgment and left.

"I'll meet you on the beach," Daniel thought to Mallie.

They both appeared on the beach instantly. Daniel quickly pulled Mallie into his arms and kissed her.

"Ummm, that's nice," said Mallie.

"Yeah," agreed Daniel snuggling his nose into her neck and holding her closely.

"What did you find out?" asked Mallie.

"Well, I found out the technician has the hots for the nurse, but she is giving him the cold shoulder. That's about it. The doctor is the only one with answers. I don't know when he will show up. I'll just have to wait, like the rest of my family. I feel fine, though."

"Me, too, but we are still both in comas." Mallie ended on a despondent note.

"We are alright. I don't know what will happen if we don't both wake up. It scares me to think of losing you." Daniel drew her close and held her gently.

"You are not going to lose me and I am not going to lose you. We are going to be together." Mallie declared fiercely.

"I love you," declared Daniel. "Without you I would have no life."

"I love you, too." said Mallie. "We will be together. Remember you promised me a daughter."

Daniel chuckled as he held on to Mallie.

CHAPTER 9

he Grey family was sitting around in Daniel's room talking. When the doctor had not made it by lunch time, Matt was getting anxious. When his phone rang, he answered it quickly.

"Hello, I'll be right there." He hung up the phone and looked at all of the scrutinizing faces. "I'll be back in a little while. I'm meeting Barbara in the cafeteria for lunch." With a quick wave he was out the door before anyone could say anything.

Matt hurried down to find Barbara just about to enter the cafeteria. He took her hand and entered with her. They took their places in line to get their lunch. "I'm very glad you agreed to have lunch with me," he told Barbara.

"I'm glad you asked me." Barbara smiled at him.

Matt reached around Barbara and paid for both of their lunches. They looked around and spotted an empty table by the window. Matt led the way to it. After they were seated and starting on their lunch, Barbara kept taking quick looks at Matt. Most of the time, she would catch Matt her looking back at her.

"When will you be home again?" asked Barbara.

"I don't know, yet. I am going to be back in the States in a month, but I don't know where I will be stationed. Now I have met you, I'm going to come home for a visit as soon as I can." Matt looked at her earnestly. "I intend to see if we can build on the feelings we are sharing. I know I have never felt this way before, and I want it to last."

"You know," said Barbara. "I had a terrible crush on you when I was a teenager. I don't think I ever got over it."

Matt took her hand and squeezed it lightly. He kept her hand and didn't let go. "I'm glad."

Barbara smiled. "You know it is hard to eat with one hand."

"Eating is highly overrated," Matt held onto her hand. He raised it to his mouth and kissed it lightly.

Barbara looked around to see if anyone was watching and then decided it didn't matter. She loved the way it made her feel.

"Will you go out with me tonight when you close your bakery?" asked Matt.

"Today's my early day. We close at six. Do you want to go to a movie?"

"I can think of nothing I would like more than making out with you in a movie. I'll pick you up at six thirty. I'll even borrow a car so we won't have to worry about my driver." Matt told her enthusiastically.

"Oh, I don't know I think it is kind of neat to have a driver at your beck and call," teased Barbara.

"We can take the driver if you want to," said Matt.

"It will be even more fun to have you all to myself," she said.

Matt leaned forward and gave her a quick kiss. After taking their plates to the window, they left. Matt gave her another quick kiss before they parted.

"I'll see you tonight," he promised. They parted, Barbara going back to work and Matt back to Daniel's room.

Matt entered Daniel's room and looked around. Katie and Brian were the only ones there besides Daniel.

"Where are Mom and Dad? Has the doctor come by with any news on Daniel?" Matt asked.

"The nurse told us the doctor had an emergency and he won't be making rounds until later today. Dad went to the store and Mom went home for a rest. You sure are looking pleased with yourself. Did you have a nice lunch?" teased Katie.

"Yes, I did, Miss Nosy. I had a great lunch. Barbara and I are going to the movies tonight."

"Wow, you sure don't waste any time," exclaimed Katie.

"I don't have any time to waste. I have to use what time I have. I really like her Katie."

Katie came over and gave her big brother a hug. "I hope everything works out for you," she said

"Thanks," responded Matt.

Bob had reluctantly gone in to his office. He didn't want to leave Dana alone, but she insisted. He worked for several hours and cleared his desk. The people in the office knew he wanted to be with Dana and all of them pitched in to help lighten his load. When he prepared to leave, Jane brought in a large bouquet of flowers.

"The office workers went in together and got these flowers for Mallie. We were wondering if you would take them to Dana for us."

"I'll be glad to. I know Dana will really appreciate them. Maybe they can cheer her up. She really is worried about Mallie. It's taking so long for her to wake up." Bob took the flowers from Jane and set them on his desk so he could take them when he left.

"Tell Dana, if there is anything we can do to help to just let us know."

"I will, thank the others, and tell them Mallie is going to get better. I won't hear of anything else," said Bob fiercely.

Jane left and Bob was soon on his way back to the hospital.

"Hello," said Bob as he entered Mallie's room and found Dana holding her hand and talking to her.

Dana rose and came towards him. "Goodness, what a pretty bouquet of flowers."

"They are from the office. Jane asked me to deliver them. She also said to tell you if there is anything any of them can do, just let them know."

Dana eyes teared up. "Thank them for me."

"I already did," responded Bob.

"They are a great bunch," said Dana.

"Yes, they are and they all love Mallie. They watched her grow up."

Bob put his arm around Dana and held her closely.

"We all love you and Mallie, me most of all."

"Oh, Bob." Dana snuggled in close and laid her face on Bob's chest.

"Has there been any news while I was gone?"

"No, the doctor hasn't been by. He had an emergency and is doing his rounds later."

"Well, you don't mind if I wait with you, do you?"

"No, I am glad you are here. I am getting used to having you around. I may never let you go again," Dana teased.

"That's fine with me. I can't think of anything I would like more than being with you forever."

Bob pulled her close and lowered his head to hers for a gentle kiss. Dana tensed, then relaxed. She leaned towards him and deepened the kiss. When the kiss ended, Bob leaned in and rested his forehead on Dana's. Both he and Dana were short of breath.

"Wow, can we do that again?" asked Dana.

Bob laughed and pulled her close for another kiss. This time Dana contributed enthusiastically. Bob and Dana were sedately sitting on the couch, with his arm around her, when the doctor entered later in the afternoon. Dana quickly rose and went over to Mallie's bedside. She didn't say anything until the doctor was through with his examination. "Has there been any improvement?" she asked.

"As far as I can tell, she's doing fine. She is improving. We just have to give her time to heal."

"Thank you, Doctor," Dana said as the doctor left the room.

Dana turned into Bob's arms. "We just have to wait," she sighed.

When the doctor left Mallie's room, he went down the hall to Daniel's room. Going into Daniel's room, he went over to the bed and checked his chart. He listened to his heart and felt his skin. After he finished his examination, he turned to the anxious people in the room. Mary had returned to the hospital after going home to take a shower and freshen up. Matt, Katie and Brian were with her.

"How is he doing?" asked Mary.

"According to the x-ray, the blood clot has dissolved. His blood is flowing freely now. There don't seem to be any other clots coming from his leg. I am worried about the stroke, now. I can't be sure how much damage was done before we got the clot dissolved. I am going to schedule an EEG for tomorrow . The last one we did wasn't showing much brain activity. We will know more after the test." The doctor surprised everyone by patting Mary's arm and telling her not to worry too much. "We can be encouraged by the blood thinner working. We won't have to put a stint in." With a brief nod for the other occupants of the room, the doctor left.

"Boy, his attitude has changed," said Katie. She went to her mom and put an arm around her. "Are you alright?" she asked.

"Yes, I'm doing alright. I can't fall apart now. I have to keep believing my boy is going to get up out of that bed and go home with us. I won't accept any other outcome." She smiled. "Dana and I have been working on the doctor. It seems to have paid off. He acts much more human now."

"I'll say," responded Katie. Matt and Brian nodded in agreement with her.

Matt came around Katie and hugged his mom. "Now that the doctor has come, I'm going to take off. I need to go to the house, get some rest and freshen up before my date tonight."

"You have a date?" asked Mary.

"Yes, I'm taking Barbara to the movies. By the way, could I borrow a car? I don't want to take Barbara out with a driver in a military vehicle."

"She's a nice girl. You two have a nice time. Sure, you can borrow my car. I can get a ride with your dad or with Katie and Brian. Here, let me get you my keys." Mary went to her purse, dug out her car keys and handed them to Matt.

"Thanks, Mom." Matt leaned forward and kissed his mother on her cheek. Mary blushed at this show of affection, but she seemed pleased.

Matt left quickly. He was in a very good mood as he went downstairs to dismiss his driver until the next day. After giving the driver the night off, Matt climbed into his mother's car and headed home for some rest and a shower. He was really looking forward to his date with Barbara.

Back in Daniel's room, Katie and Brian were talking to Mary. They were trying to keep her occupied so she would not worry about Daniel so much.

Katie pulled out her cell phone and started showing her the latest pictures of Sylvia. She had pictures of her eating, playing, taking a bath, making a mess and smiling prettily for the camera. Mary was enthralled with her little granddaughter.

"She's beautiful, Mary sighed softly. "When are you going to bring her for a visit?"

"Soon, Mom. Real soon." Katie gave her mom a hug and left her looking at the pictures on the phone. Katie went to Brian and leaning into him, gave him a hug and a kiss. Brian hugged her back and returned the kiss. He held her close until she pulled away to go back to her mom.

Katie patted him on his cheek. "Thanks," she said.

"Anytime," promised Brian.

Mallie stirred. She was lying in Daniel's arms. They were in their favorite place on the beach. She and Daniel had talked and kissed until they fell asleep in each other's arms. She was feeling a little stiff, but she didn't want to wake Daniel, so she grew still again. It was heaven just to lie here in his arms. Mallie sighed softly. She was worried about how things were going to go for her and Daniel. Would they wake up? Would they get to have the life they were talking about together? She loved him so much. They had to have a chance. There was no way they could not be together. Why else would they meet like this? They were destined to be together.

"You're thinking too hard," said Daniel. "Relax."

"I'm sorry. I didn't mean to wake you." Mallie said.

"That's ok. I would rather be awake and enjoy the feel of you in my arms."

"Oh, Daniel, I feel the same way." Mallie hugged him tightly for a moment. *"I love you so much. It is hard to believe I had to be in a coma to meet the love of my life."*

"I have a feeling we were destined to meet. Fate just took over when you had your accident and I had my blood clot. Fate stepped in and brought us together." Daniel finished with satisfaction.

"Well, hurray for fate. Now it just has to wake us up so we can get started on our life together." Mallie finished tearfully.

"Shhh, it's alright we'll get our chance. I love you." Daniel soothed Mallie.

While Mallie and Daniel talked on their beach, Bob and Dana were talking in Mallie's hospital room.

"When Mallie wakes up, I'm going to take you out to celebrate. We are going to a nice restaurant, drink champagne and then we are going dancing. I want to spend a whole evening with my arms around you." Bob played with the short curls on Dana's neck as he talked.

"Are you asking me or telling me?" asked Dana. She felt a delicious shiver at the feel of Bob's hand on her neck playing with her hair.

Bob smiled. "A little of both I guess. You will go out with me, won't you?"

Dana smiled back at him. "Just as soon as Mallie wakes up, I'll be glad to go out with you. I would love to go dancing. I haven't done that in years. It will be wonderful to go again and being with you will make it better."

Bob pulled her closer and gave her a gentle kiss.

"How do I get Mallie to hurry and wake up?" he asked teasingly.

"If I knew how to do that, I would have already had her awake." Dana replied. She lay her head against Bob's chest and relaxed.

Bob closed his arms around her and nuzzled his chin in her hair.

"She will wake up, soon," he replied.

Matt decided to walk over to Barbara's house to get her instead of moving the car. When he knocked on the door, Barbara's mother opened it. She looked at him enquiringly.

"Hello, Mrs. Smith. I'm Matt Grey from next door. I'm here to pick up Barbara. We are going to the movies."

Mrs. Smith smiled as she opened the screen door for Matt. "Hello, Matt. I haven't seen you in ages." She led the way into the living room and indicated the sofa. "Have a seat. Barbara will be down shortly. She hasn't been home from work for very long. How is Daniel doing?"

Matt obligingly sat on the sofa. "Daniel is still in a coma, but the clot has been dissolved, so we are hoping he will to wake up soon."

Barbara came in the room as he gave her mother this news. "Hi" she greeted Matt.

"Hi," Matt stood up as he greeted Barbara. "are you ready to go?"

"Yes" she replied. She turned and gave her mom a quick hug. "Good night, Mom. I'll see you later."

She and Matt walked towards the door. When they got outside, Matt began to lead her next door. She looked at him, puzzled. Matt chuckled at her look. "I thought I would leave the car there and walk over to get you. You don't mind a short walk, do you?"

"No, I don't mind," She agreed.

When they got to the car, Matt opened her door and waited for her to get in before shutting the door and rounding the car to the driver's side. "Would you like to stop and get something to eat before the movie?" asked Matt.

"No," replied Barbara. "I just want a large bucket of popcorn for us to share and large drinks."

"The only way to see a movie," agreed Matt.

"Do you know which movie you want to see?"

"I don't know what's playing. We can decide when we get there."

"Ok," agreed Matt.

They decided on a 3D version of Transformers.

"Are you sure you want to watch this movie?" asked Matt.

"Absolutely," declared Barbara with a big grin. "Let's get our popcorn."

"Ok," agreed Matt.

They got their popcorn and drinks and took seats about halfway down in the theater. They settled in to watch the previews while they waited for the movie to start. When they announced the movie starting, Matt handed Barbara her 3D glasses. Barbara took them with a smile. "I love 3D movies," she said.

They dug into their popcorn and prepared to watch the movie. Matt put his arm around Barbara and smiled at her enthusiasm.

"Oh, look, the robots look like they are coming out into the theater." Barbara ducked her head as if dodging the robot.

Matt laughed and held her tighter. "I can see definite advantages to a 3D movie," he said.

"Yeah," agreed Barbara as she snuggled closer to Matt.

"Like I said, I love 3D movies." She smiled up at Matt. He leaned forward and kissed her lightly.

"Ummm, good," said Barbara. "You taste just like popcorn."

Everyone in the audience gasped and Barbara quickly looked back at the movie. Matt settled back, holding Barbara and enjoying the movie with her.

After the movie was over, Matt and Barbara gathered their cups and popcorn bucket to deposit in the trash can. Barbara wanted to keep the 3D glasses as a souvenir, so Matt stuck them in his pocket to keep for her.

"I had a very good time tonight," said Barbara. "I'm glad we settled on that movie."

"Me, too," said Matt. "I haven't enjoyed a movie this much since I was a kid. The company was great, also." He turned her to face him and took a quick kiss. He leaned back and looked into her eyes. "I am falling in love with you," he said.

"I'm glad," replied Barbara. "Because, I love you, too."

Matt leaned down for another kiss.

They were interrupted by catcalls and whistles from a passing car. Matt drew back, reluctantly. He looked around as if just remembering being on a public street.

"We had better go," he said. He held Barbara close to his side as they continued towards their car.

"I only have a few more days before I have to report for duty. Is there any chance we could get together when I come back? Would you write to me? I don't know what else I can do without rushing you. I don't want to scare you away, but I do want us to consider making a life together. I don't know how, yet. We'll have to work on the details." Matt paused for breath. Barbara put a hand over his lips.

"Will you pause long enough for me to answer? Yes, we can get together anytime you want. Yes, I will write to you. You are not rushing me or scaring me. I have been in love with you forever. I hope we can work out the details because I do want a life with you."

Matt pulled Barbara into his arms for a passionate kiss. When he came up for air, they were both breathing hard.

Matt groaned. "We are still on a public street. We had better go before we get arrested for improper behavior."

He helped Barbara into the car and drove home. He parked in his parents' driveway and reached for Barbara. It was quite a while before he walked her to her home next door.

CHAPTER 10

*D*aniel was already on the beach before he called for Mallie. He didn't see any need to go down to x-ray where they were doing the EEG. He would much rather be on the beach with Mallie.

Mallie appeared instantly and burrowed into Daniel.

"I am so glad you called. I feel like a peeping tom in the room with Mom and Bob. I am glad those two are getting together, but I don't want to listen.

Daniel chuckled. "I'm glad they are getting together, too. It will make it much easier for us. You are going to marry me, aren't you?" He looked into her face enquiringly.

"Yes," responded Mallie. "I want us to be married as soon as possible so that we can start working on the little girl you promised me."

Mallie looked into Daniel's eyes. "I love you very much," she said.

"I love you, too." Daniel leaned closer and started a soft kiss. It soon became much more and left them both breathless.

~

Daniel was down in x-ray for about an hour, before they brought him back to his room. Katie, Matt and Mary were waiting.. Herman had to go to his store and Brian had some work on the computer that had to be finished. They had learned that it would do no good to ask any questions. They had to wait for the doctor to find out anything.

Katie wandered over to the window and stood looking out. Matt joined her there. Katie turned and looked at Matt.

"You and Barbara are getting close pretty fast. Don't you have to leave in a few more days?"

Matt sighed. "Yeah, we talked about it. She's going to write and I will try to be stationed close by as soon as I get transferred back to the States. I really care about her, Katie. I want to make a life with her."

Katie gave her brother a hug. "Well, you go for it. Don't let anything stand in your way. I hope everything works out for you."

"Thanks, I hope so, too."

Matt looked over at his mother. She was at Daniel's bedside, with her eyes closed, saying a prayer. Matt looked back at Katie. "I think I'll go down to the cafeteria and get some coffee. Would you like anything?"

"No, I'm fine for now. I'll go down and eat when Brian gets here," replied Katie.

Matt left without disturbing his mother. He really just wanted to walk around a bit and stretch his legs. He was not accustomed to sitting so much. Matt got his coffee and looked around for a seat. He saw Dana and Bob at a table by the window. Walking over, he decided to say hello. Dana looked up and smiled when he stopped by their table.

"Hi, I saw the two of you sitting here and I thought I would ask how Mallie is doing."

"Have a seat. Mallie is about the same. We left her with the nurse who gives her a bath and massage," Dana answered.

Matt pulled out a chair and sat. "It is so hard just watching them lay there," sighed Matt. "I look at my little brother and I want to say come on wake up, Daniel. He should be out, living his, life not lying there so still."

"I know," agreed Dana.

Matt looked over at Bob. "I hear you are the local realtor. Are there any good bargains in homes around here?"

"Well, it would depend on what you are looking for," said Bob. "We have a new subdivision going in just West of town. There are some older homes scattered around. Are you looking to buy a home around here?"

"I'm thinking about it," Matt answered.

"Well, when you get ready just come on by and we will set you up in your dream home." Bob handed Matt his card.

Matt took the card and looked at it. "I just might. Matt rose from his seat. I guess I had better get back upstairs. It was nice talking to you."

"See you later," answered Dana.

Matt left and Bob retrieved Dana's hand. He couldn't seem to go long without touching her. Dana smiled at him, but she left her hand in his.

The nurse was just getting ready to leave when Bob and Dana returned to Mallie's room.

"I think there was a small reaction when I was massaging Mallie's foot. I can't be sure. It was like it tensed for a few seconds. Maybe she is getting aware of things. We'll just have to wait and see." With this cheerful news, the nurse left.

"I am getting so tired of those words," said Dana. "Wait and see is all I have been doing."

"The news is encouraging," said Bob. "If Mallie is getting some sensation back, she must be coming out of the coma."

"You're right. After all of this, I don't need to start getting picky." She turned her face into Bob's chest. "Oh, Bob, my little girl may be waking up."

Bob held her closely and shared the happy moment with her.

In Daniel's room Mary, Brian, and Matt waited anxiously for the results of the EEG. Katie had gone outside to call and check on Sylvia. Brian and Matt sat by the window and talked quietly while Mary held Daniel's hand and prayed for him. They all came to their feet when the doctor entered the room. The doctor went to the bed to check on Daniel and read his chart. The doctor turned toward Mary when he finished checking Daniel.

"The EEG did not show any signs of any additional trouble with blood clots. The only problem is there is limited brain activity. So far, he does not seem to be emerging from the coma. There is no way to tell if he will ever come out of the coma. We will keep monitoring him to see if there is any increase in brain activity. For the time being that's all we can do. I'm sorry," He told Mary as he squeezed her hand.

Mary managed a weak smile. "Thank you, Doctor. I know you are doing all you can." The doctor gave her hand another squeeze and then left.

After he was gone, Matt noticed that his mother was crying. He went over and took her into his arms.

"Come on, Mom, you can't give up hope. Depend on Daniel. He will come back to us. You have to have faith. Don't let some stupid machine make you give up. Come on, give me a smile and show me some of that famous fighting spirit of yours."

Mary gave Matt a tremulous smile. "You're right we can't rule out Daniel just because of a test. He is flesh and blood. We have to hope for a miracle. Daniel will come back to us," She gave one last sniff and patted Matt's chest.

"Thanks for reminding me," she said.

"You're welcome," said Matt.

Mary went back to Daniel's bedside and resumed her prayers.

Daniel and Mallie were oblivious to the turmoil going on in their rooms. Mallie had no idea about the nurse detecting sensation in her foot and Daniel didn't know about the EEG results. They were both oblivious to the outside world. Their world, at the moment, consisted of the two of them. They didn't want any intruders.

"*I have been thinking about a name for our daughter,*" *said Mallie.*

"*Aren't you getting a little ahead of things here?*" *asked Daniel.*

"*No,*" *said Mallie.* "*You have to plan ahead for these things.*"

"*Ok,*" *said Daniel indulgently.* "*What did you come up with?*"

"*Well,*" *said Mallie.* "*I think we should name her Mary Danielle.*" *She looked at Daniel expectantly.* "*What do you think?*"

Daniel looked at her with tears in his eyes. "I think it's a great name and Mom will love it."

"We could call her Dani. That way no one will get their feelings hurt."

"I love you," said Daniel. He held her closely and showed her how much.

Mallie returned his kiss with enthusiasm.

"I guess we need to go and see what's going on," said Daniel.

"I guess, so," said Mallie with a sigh. "Let me know what the doctor says about yourEEG."

"Ok" Daniel gave her another quick kiss and they vanished to their respective rooms.

Mallie listened to Dana and Bob discussing the nurse's words. She wondered if it could be true. Wouldn't she have felt something if the sensation was coming back? She had felt it when they gave her the shots. Maybe the shots were felt because they hurt.

"Daniel," she thought.

"I'm here, Mallie," Daniel answered. "Is anything wrong?"

"No, I was just listening to Mom and Bob. They said the nurse thought she felt some movement in my foot. Could there be sensation in my foot and I not know it?"

"I don't know. Do you feel anything in your foot now? Can you move it?"

Mallie tried concentrating on her foot, trying to make it move.

"It doesn't do anything but lay there. I can't move it."

"Well, maybe she was mistaken. It will happen Mallie, just be patient."

"Have you heard anything about yourtest?"

"No, not yet. I'll let you know when I do."

"OK," Mallie said

Daniel began listening as his mom and Katie came into the room. They must have gone to the cafeteria.

"Has anything happened?" Mary asked Matt.

"No," Matt replied everything has been quiet since the doctor came by. "Did you have a nice meal?"

"Yes, I did. I don't think Katie enjoyed it as much as I did. They had meat loaf. I have always been fond of meat loaf. It's has never been Katie's favorite meal." Mary answered.

Herman entered the room and Mary turned to face him. She went over, buried her face in his chest and held on tight. Herman closed his arms around Mary and looked toward Matt and Brian.

"What's wrong? Has something happened?" he asked.

"The doctor came by with the results of the EEG. He said there was very little brain activity. He didn't seem to know what the cause was or if it would change. He said they would have to keep an eye on him." Matt explained to Herman. Herman held on to Mary. His face looked as if he were in pain.

"Mallie," thought Daniel.

"I'm here, Daniel," Mallie thought.

"The doctor told the family my test showed very little brain activity."

Mallie thought for a minute.

"Of course," she thought. "There was little brain activity because you weren't there. You were on the beach with me."

Daniel thought about it. "You could be right. Next time they do an EEG I'll have to go along for the ride and see if there is any difference."

"I know I'm right," Mallie insisted. "You'll see."

Daniel chuckled. "Get some rest, Mallie. I'll talk to you later."

"Goodnight, Daniel," she replied.

Herman persuaded Mary to go home for a rest. He went with her to make sure she was alright. He left Matt and Brian with Daniel. He gave them instructions to call him if there was any change. They both promised faithfully to call. He and Mary had not been gone long when Matt's phone rang. Matt looked surprised when he recognized the number. He went out in the hall to take the call. With all of the machinery in Daniel's room, cell phones were not allowed to be answered in there.

"Hello," answered Matt.

Matt listened to the speaker for a minute.

"Yes, Sir, I'll see you at Oh-thirteen-hundred tomorrow."

Matt hung up the phone and re-entered Daniel's room.

"I have to go to the base tomorrow at one pm," he told Brian.

"Is there a problem?" asked Brian.

"I don't know. Major Davis had his office call me and ask me to come in. I guess I will find out when I get there."

As soon as Katie came back with the coffee for her and Brian, Matt slipped out again to call Barbara.

"Hello," answered Barbara. "Smith's Bakery."

"Hi, do you think you could come by the hospital after you get off work?" Matt asked.

"Sure," answered Barbara. "Has something happened?"

"There has been no change in Daniel's condition. Dad took Mom home to rest. She was getting pretty emotional. I think she just needed to get away from the stress for a while."

"Ok, I'll be closing at six thirty. I'll see you soon."

"Bye, I love you," said Matt.

"Bye, I love you, too," said Barbara.

Matt went back inside to keep Katie and Brian company while he waited for evening and Barbara.

Katie and Brian looked up as Matt returned to Daniel's room. "I bet you have been talking to Barbara," she teased.

"Why do you say that?" asked Matt.

"Well, maybe it's the satisfied look you have on your face, or it could be you looking so much more relaxed." Katie observed.

Brian chuckled. "You can't put anything over on Katie. She has all the instincts of a female. They are very observant when it comes to love." He gave Katie a hug.

Matt laughed. "Yes, I was talking to Barbara. She's going to stop by here when she closes her bakery."

Katie wandered over to Daniel's bedside. She stood looking down at him for a minute and took his hand, giving it a squeeze. Then she lay his hand back on the bed and turned around. Brian, seeing the tears starting to form in his wife's eyes, quickly rose and went to her side. He put his arm around her shoulders and gave her a brief squeeze.

"How was Sylvia doing when you talked to her earlier? Has she been getting into everything and running Mom ragged?"

Katie face instantly cleared. There was nothing that cheered her up faster than thinking about her daughter.

"Your mom said she has been a little angel. Of course, we know better. Sylvia can try the patience of a saint sometimes, but she makes up for it when she cuddles closely and rains kisses on your face." Katie sighed. "I hope Daniel gets better, soon. I miss my little girl."

"Yeah," agreed Brian. "I miss her, too."

"Ok you two, lighten up. Sylvia is being spoiled rotten and you'll be back with her, soon." Matt said. "Daniel is going to get up out of this hospital bed and get on with his life." Matt looked over at Daniel with a prayer in his heart.

After the drama, the three of them sat quietly talking. Katie pulled out her phone and showed Matt the pictures of Sylvia. He didn't seem to mind looking at them again. He even laughed at some of the messier ones. They had been so engrossed, they looked up in surprise when the door opened and Barbara entered.

Matt quickly rose and went to her, pulling her towards him for a kiss. Barbara hid her face against his chest when the kiss ended.

"We have an audience," she whispered.

"I don't care," said Matt. "I already told Brian and Katie I love you. They are not surprised."

Barbara peeped around Matt at Katie. "You don't mind?" she asked.

Katie quickly came over to Barbara. "I think it's wonderful. You will make a wonderful sister. I always thought so. I used to pretend you were my sister. Now you will be. I'm really glad you and Matt got together."

"Thank you," said Barbara. "I have always wanted you for a sister. I'm glad it's going to be a reality."

"Me, too," agreed Katie.

"Would you like to go down to the cafeteria? We can get something to eat or just coffee?" Matt enquired.

"Sure," Barbara responded.

"We will see you guys in a little while," Matt told Katie and Brian as they left.

Matt and Barbara went through the cafeteria line and decided they would keep their meal light. Neither of them was very hungry. After seating themselves at their favorite table by the window, Barbara looked at Matt.

"Ok," she said. "What's going on?"

"I'm that obvious, am I?" said Matt.

Barbara shrugged as she waited for Matt to speak.

"I received a call from my commander. It was just from his

office so I don't know what he wants. I am to report to his office at one o' clock tomorrow. I'll have to catch a flight out in the morning. I am hoping I'll be back tomorrow night, but I can't be sure. I'll get back as soon as I can."

Barbara sighed. "I guess I will have to get used to things like this if I'm going to be the wife of a Marine."

Matt took her hand. "You are going to be the wife of a Marine. I love you. We'll make it work, somehow."

"I'm not complaining. I love you, too. I want our lives together to start as soon as possible. We'll work things out. Don't worry." She gave Matt's hand a reassuring squeeze.

Matt and Barbara ate their meal and went back up to Daniel's room.

When they entered the room the first thing they saw was a large bouquet of flowers.

"Wow," said Matt. "Where did those come from?"

"They were delivered right after you left. Take a look at the card." said Katie.

Matt crossed over to the flowers and leaned down to get a look at the card.

"They are from Major Davis' office. Wow, I didn't know the Marine Corps did things like this!" exclaimed Matt.

Matt looked around. "I was thinking, has the fancy law firm Daniel works for asked about him or been in touch at all?"

"Not since I've been here. I don't know about before. You would have to ask Mom. I don't really want to upset her any more than she already is," said Katie.

"You're right. It can wait. I was just curious." Matt sat down on the couch and tugged Barbara down beside him.

CHAPTER 11

"*Mallie*," *thought Daniel.*

"*I'm here,*" *answered Mallie.*

"*I was just listening to Matt and Katie talk and I just real-ized something.*"

"*What's that?*" *Mallie encouraged him to continue.*

"*No one from the law firm has asked about me since I collapsed in the office.*" *Daniel replied.*

"*What a bunch of jerks. You need to get away from those people, Daniel,*" *Mallie was very indignant on his behalf.*

Daniel laughed. "I didn't mean to get you stirred up, but I think you are right. I have already been thinking about it. I just don't know what I can do. I am going to have to work, so we can be married. I have to plan for little Dani."

Mallie chuckled. "I have been thinking about this. Did you study real estate law in school?"

"*Sure, it was included in my studies, why?*"

"*I heard Bob complaining several times about always having to get an attorney for any legal work done on sales. I bet he would love having his own in-house attorney." Mallie finished smugly.*

"I don't know, Mallie. We will have to wait until we wake up and check it out."

"Ok," agreed Mallie. "Is anything else going on? Mom and Bob can't keep their hands off of each other. I'm pretty sure I'm going to have a stepfather, soon."

"Matt has to report in to his base tomorrow and his commanding officer sent a large bouquet of flowers. I could hear Katie drooling over them."

"Ohhh, I wish I could see them," said Mallie.

"They are just flowers," responded Daniel.

"Daniel Grey, there is no such thing as 'just flowers.' Flowers are unique and beautiful. It makes your heart flutter to get a large sweet-smelling bouquet."

"I'll have to remember to get you lots of flowers." Daniel sighed. "I want you to be happy, Mallie."

"Oh, Daniel I don't need flowers to make me happy. I just need you."

Daniel could feel his eyes moisten. "I love you, Mallie. You are all I have ever wanted or needed."

Mallie felt her own eyes moisten. "Good night, Daniel."

"Good night, Mallie."

Herman and Mary came back at just before midnight.

"You did not have to come back tonight, Mom. Brian and I would be glad to stay. Why don't you sleep in your bed tonight?" Katie appealed to her mom.

"I tried to get her to stay home tonight," Herman shook his head. "She had to come back. Why don't you and Brian go and get some rest? You and Barbara can go too, Matt."

"I have to take Barbara home," said Matt. "I will be flying to headquarters in the morning."

"Why?" asked Mary. "I thought you had a week."

"I do," explained Matt. "Major Davis' office called. He wants to see me. I won't know why until I get there. Did you see the flowers Major Davis sent?"

"Oh, they're beautiful," said Mary going over for a closer look at the flowers.

Katie gave her parents a hug. Brian gave Mary a hug and shook Herman's hand. "Good night," said Katie. "If you need us, just call."

"Ok," said Herman. "goodnight."

Matt said goodnight to his family, and he and Barbara left. Herman and Mary settled down for the night.

.

Corporal James was waiting for them at the front door. When he dropped them at home, Matt told him he had to be at the airport in the morning. Corporal James enquired as to the destination. "I'm going to headquarters," Matt answered.

"Well, Captain, we have transport leaving for headquarters at Oh-eight-hundred. You could catch a ride if you want."

"I certainly do want the ride. Thanks." said Matt.

"Alright," said the grinning Corporal James. "see you in the morning." With a salute, which Matt returned, he drove away.

Matt walked Barbara home. At her door he stopped and drew her close to him for a goodnight kiss. They were both slightly breathless when the kiss ended.

"I had better go," said Matt.

"Call me when you find out what's going on," said Barbara.

"I will," promised Matt.

"Goodnight." After another quick kiss he turned for home and Barbara went inside.

Matt knocked at Major Davis' office door and at one minute before Oh-thirteen-hundred-hours. When he heard "Come in", he entered, stood at attention, and saluted the major. Major Davis stood and returned his salute.

"At ease, have a seat Captain."

Matt took the chair indicated and seated himself.

"How is your brother," Major Davis questioned.

"There's been no change, Sir. He's still in a coma." Matt replied.

"I'm sorry to hear that."

"Thank you for the flowers. My mother loved them."

"You're welcome. The Marine Corps is like a family. You are a Marine. That makes your brother part of our family. When I find out who did not pass your mother's message to you, well, let's just say it won't happen again. I noticed that you have two years left on your enlistment."

"Yes, Sir," replied Matt.

"You had one month left on your overseas assignment. I decided to expedite it and have you transferred back early. I thought you would like to be closer to your family at this time. Anything left in your room will be packed and sent here, where we will forward it to you. Is that all satisfactory to you, Captain?"

"Yes, Sir, I was not looking forward to leaving before my brother wakes from his coma. I really appreciate this." Matt sat waiting for what else the Major had to say.

The Major studied Matt for a moment before he continued. "I could have handled this by phone, but I wanted to see you, face to face, when we talked. I wanted you to understand you are in no way obligated to take up my suggestion. If you have something else in mind, I will listen and see what I can do." Major Davis paused and gave Matt time to respond.

"Yes, Sir," said Matt. "I understand."

"Have you given any thought to what you want to do when your tour overseas is finished?"

"Yes, Sir, I would like to be closer to home. I don't know what is available, yet. I haven't been looking."

"Have you considered recruitment?"

"What does a person in recruitment have to do?" asked Matt.

"A recruiter mans the recruitment office. He travels to high schools and talks to seniors. He sets up booths at job fairs and just gets the Marine Corp message out to the public. Do you think you would be interested?"

"Yes, Sir, I'm interested. Where would I be stationed?"

"We have a recruitment officer getting ready to retire for health reasons. He needs a replacement as soon as possible. The only thing is you only have two years left on your enlistment and one of the requirements is for a five-year commitment. The office is in your home town."

The Major looked at Matt, who was trying to contain his excitement.

"Well, do I start the paperwork?' He asked.

"Yes, Sir, I am ready anytime. Thank you, Sir."

"Ok, I'll start on it and I'll be in touch in about a week with some papers for you to sign."

The Major stood and Matt rose also.

"Good luck Captain."

With another salute exchanged he dismissed Matt from his office.

Matt waited until he was outside the hanger, waiting for the transport to be ready to take off, to call Barbara.

"Hello, Smith's Bakery," answered Barbara.

"Hello, beautiful. I love you," Matt answered.

"I love you, too. Have you seen the Major?"

"Yes, I just came from there. I'm at the transport now, waiting for take-off."

"Well," said Barbara. "What did the Major want?"

Matt laughed. "He wanted to tell me he had expedited my return to the States so that I do not have to go overseas."

"That's wonderful!" exclaimed Barbara. "Did he say anything about where you are going to be stationed next?"

"Yes, but I will have to explain it to you when I get back. The transport is ready to go. I have to board. I love you."

Matt hung up the phone and hurried to board the transport. If his smile got any brighter, they would be able to see it shine all the way to Denton.

Barbara hung up her phone and turned to her assistant, Lucy.

"If the smile on your face is anything to go by, I'd say you just had some good news." Lucy said.

"The best," agreed Barbara. "Matt doesn't have to go back overseas."

"Where will he be going?" inquired Lucy.

"I don't know. He had to catch a plane. He said he would explain all when he gets back here. I can't wait." Barbara exclaimed. "At least he will be here in the states where we can see each other."

She hurried into the back room to check on some donuts. Her assistant smiled indulgently.

It was about five o' clock when Matt landed back in Denton. He had Corporal James drive him straight to Barbara's Bakery. He was so excited he could not wait for closing time.

Barbara ran into his arms as soon as he entered the bakery. After a hug and a very satisfying kiss, Barbara leaned back in his arms and got a good look at his face.

"Tell me you have good news," she said.

"I have great news," declared Matt. "I am going to be stationed at the recruiting office here in Denton."

"What!" Barbara squealed. She flung her arms back around Matt and squeezed hard. "If I am dreaming, please don't wake me up."

"You're not dreaming. Major Davis is getting the paperwork in order. All I have to do is sign and it is a done deal. I have to sign up for an additional three years, but I don't mind that."

"It will mean job security for at least the next five years." agreed Barbara.

"It also means we can be married. We are going to start making plans and looking for a house just as soon as everything is signed and set. I already have a card from Bob Jenkins Realty. We can give him a call and see what is available."

"I am so excited I can hardly stand it," said Barbara. "Have you told your folks?"

"No, I came straight here. Are you through here? We could tell them together."

"You guys go on. I can close up," said Lucy.

"Are you sure you don't mind?" asked Barbara.

"Its fine, now git. Congratulations."

"Ok," agreed Barbara. She took off her apron and she and Matt left to go to the hospital.

Katie and Brian took one look at Matt and Barbara's smiling faces when they entered Daniel's room and knew they had some good news.

"Well, big brother, what's going on? Katie asked, as she

looked from one to the other "If you two smile any brighter we won't need a light in here tonight.".

Matt pulled Barbara in closer to his side. "This wonderful lady has consented to be my wife,"

Katie gave a squeal of delight and ran over to hug Barbara.

"Congratulations," said Brian as he shook Matt's hand and hugged Barbara. Katie's squeal had drawn Mary and Herman's attention away from Daniel and over to them. They looked at Katie quizzically.

"Matt and Barbara are getting married," she explained.

Mary came over and hugged Matt and Barbara. Herman also offered his congratulations to both.

"Don't you have to leave, soon?" asked Herman.

"That's what Major Davis wanted to see me about," explained a grinning Matt. "He expedited my transfer and I don't have to go back overseas. I will be staying in the States."

There was another round of hugs and congratulations.

"Where will you be stationed?" asked Mary.

"That's another part of the good news. I'm being transferred to the recruitment office here in Denton."

Matt took his Mom in his arms for a hug as she started to cry. "I thought it was good news," Matt responded.

"It is great news. I'm just so happy. I can't help crying," said Mary.

They all started talking at once and it was such a joyous time they forgot about Daniel and his coma for a little while. Matt and Barbara left to go and break the news to Barbara's family. Katie and Brian decided to go and check on Sylvia. Mary and Herman were left with Daniel.

"Our family is growing," said Mary.

"Yes, it will be good to have them all close again," said Herman.

"Now, if Daniel would just wake up everything would be perfect," sighed Mary.

Herman put his arm around Mary's shoulder. "He will wake up. It will happen," he said fiercely.

Mary turned and buried her face in Herman's chest. "I can't lose my baby," she whispered.

"I know, I know," agreed Herman.

Daniel had called for Mallie and they met on their private beach. After a very satisfactory greeting they seated themselves with Mallie leaning back in Daniel's arms.

"What is happening?" asked Mallie.

"My brother, Matt and his girl, Barbara, are getting married. His Major had him transferred back to the states and he will be running the recruitment office here in Denton. Everyone is very happy and celebrating."

"That's good news," said Mallie. "Aren't you happy for them?"

"Yeah, I'm glad for them. I just wish I could wake up and celebrate with them."

"We will wake up, and they will have our wedding to celebrate, too." Mallie said as she hugged Daniel and tried to cheer him up.

"I am looking forward to it," said Daniel. He pulled Mallie closer to him and rested his chin on her head.

"Has the nurse felt any more movement from your feet?" asked Daniel.

"I don't think so. If she had, she hasn't said anything about it." Mallie replied.

"I think they are taking me down for another EEG in the

morning. I'm going to stay this time and see if it makes any difference," Daniel said thoughtfully.

"Let me know as soon as you find anything out," Mallie said.

"I will," promised Daniel.

~

Daniel and Mallie returned to their rooms early the next morning so Daniel would be there when the nurse came to take him down for another test. Mallie found Dana and Bob getting ready to go down to the cafeteria. The nurse was waiting for them to leave to give Mallie her bath and Massage.

"We'll be right down in the cafeteria," reminded Dana.

"You two go ahead. Everything will be fine here," The nurse ushered them out of Mallie's room.

After they were gone, the nurse prepared the water and soap for the bath. She sat the pan on Mallie's bedside table and pulled the sheet back to start the bath. She then turned to get the washcloth. When the cold air hit Mallie's skin, she shivered. The nurse turned back with the cloth and noticed goosebumps on Mallie's skin. She smiled.

"That's a good sign," she said.

The nurse quickly gave Mallie her bath so that she could get her covered up. She then uncovered Mallie's legs and started massaging them. She rubbed them with oil and massaged them, and then started on her arms. When she was finished, she covered Mallie and gathered together everything she had been using, cleaning up the area as she went.

"Well," she said. "You are good for another day. I think you are getting better. It won't be long before you won't have any need of me." She patted Mallie's arm and, smiling, left the room.

~

The nurse came for Daniel to take him down for his EEG shortly after he had his bath and massage. Mary and Herman had gone home for a rest and to clean up. Katie and Brian were there. They had waited in the cafeteria while Daniel had his bath and massage, but were back in his room now. They watched as the nurse wheeled Daniel out.

"Do you think Matt will be here, soon?" asked Katie.

He waited at the house to speak with your parents before coming in. He'll be here, soon." Brian reassured her.

Katie smiled. "Sylvia will look so cute in a little flower girl dress."

"You had better wait until you know what their plans are before making any plans to buy dresses," stated Brian.

Katie frowned at him. "I wasn't going to run out and start buying dresses. I will talk to Barbara first." She informed him.

Brian held up his hand. "Ok, I surrender. I will be glad to see you and Sylvia in new dresses anytime."

"I love you," said Katie as she came over and gave Brian a kiss.

"I love you, too," Brian agreed.

They waited in Daniel's room for about an hour for him to return.

Thirty minutes into their wait Matt entered.

"Good morning," said Katie. "How are mom and Dad doing?'

"They're fine. We talked about wedding plans for a while and then Dad persuaded Mom to lie down for a while. She was asleep when I left," Matt replied.

"What wedding plans have been decided?" probed Katie. Brian chuckled.

"Barbara's folks are members of the local golf club. They

want to have the reception there. We are going to try to have the ceremony in Mom's church. Everything else is pretty much on hold until I get my orders and we can set a date. I called Bob Jenkins Realty this morning and told Bob to be on the look-out for a house for us. Everything is going smoothly now. I hope it stays that way."

"Well," said Katie. "You summed everything up smoothly. I'll have to call Barbara for more details."

"I just gave you the details," said a puzzled Matt.

"Men," snorted Katie.

Brian chuckled again at the look on Matt's face. "Just go with the flow, Brother. It will make everything so much easier."

Matt didn't say anything, he just gave Katie a strange look. He then shrugged his shoulders. He wasn't going to let anything disturb him. He was too happy.

CHAPTER 12

The nurse was gone when Dana and Bob returned to Mallie's room, so they didn't get a chance to ask how she was doing. Dana walked over to Mallie's bedside. She took her hand and gave it a squeeze.

"Mallie, I love you. Please wake up. You are going to be so far behind in your nursing classes. You may have to take the rest of this semester off and start back next semester," Dana sighed. "I don't care about classes. I just want you to be back here with us. You have to be here for mine and Bob's wedding. You are going to have a stepfather, Mallie. You have to wake up and tell me what you think about it. Bob loves you, too. He will make a wonderful husband and stepfather. Please Mallie, come back to us."

Bob put his arm around Dana and held her close to his side. She turned her face into his chest and stifled her tears.

The doctor entered Mallie's room. He went to check her chart. After looking at it, the doctor smiled.

"It seems as if Mallie may be surfacing. She had a reaction to cold this morning. It seems she is becoming more aware."

"Does it mean she's going to wake up soon?" she asked.

"It means the outlook is more promising," the doctor replied.

"Thank the Lord," replied Dana.

"Yes, indeed," said the doctor.

The doctor left them with their renewed hopes and went down to Daniel's room. He entered Daniel's room and went to his chart. He read the chart and checked Daniel out.

"This EEG was more promising. He showed more brain activity. His massage therapist said there was no additional response in his legs or arms, but they are responding well to therapy. There has been no deterioration. We are hopeful he will start responding to stimuli."

With these words of encouragement, the doctor departed.

All of Daniel's family were gathered in Daniel's room they were sitting around talking, mostly about Barbara and Matt's wedding. Barbara had joined them after closing her bakery. All of a sudden, the alarms above Daniel's head started sounding.

The nurse rushed into the room followed quickly by another nurse and then the doctor. They all rushed to Daniel's bedside and started working with the controls. The doctor was checking his wiring. They were all trying to find out what the problem was. Daniel's family were all in shock. They stayed back out of the way and let the doctor and nurses work.

"Daniel," called Mallie in her mind. She called him again but it seemed as if he was retreating farther away from her.

Mallie sat up in bed with her eyes wide open.

"No," she yelled. She took the IV out of her arm and unhooked the wires from her. She sprang from her bed and, before an astonished Dana and Bob could get to her, she dashed out of the door and ran down the hall to Daniel's room. She hurried into his room and to the astonishment of everyone there, rushed to Daniel's bedside. She climbed up on the bed and straddled Daniel. Taking his shoulders in her hands, she gave them a firm shake. "Daniel Grey don't you dare leave me. I know you can hear me. I love you. Fight for us Daniel. Fight for our love. Fight, Daniel, Fight." She punctuated these words with more shakes to his shoulders.

The doctor put his hand on Mallie's shoulder. "You need to come down from there young lady," he said.

Mallie looked over her shoulder at the doctor. "Get your hand off of me," she snarled. She then ignored the doctor and turned back to Daniel.

"Please Daniel you have to fight your way back. Fight for our love. Fight for our future little girl. Fight Daniel." With this she laid her face on his chest and burst into tears.

To the astonishment of everyone in the room, including Dana and Bob who had followed her from her room, Daniel's arms started to rise until they settled around Mallie.

"Mallie love, why are you crying? What's wrong?" Daniel whispered.

Mallie became still and looked at Daniel, whose eyes were open and looking back at her.

"Daniel, I love you." She started raining kisses all over his face.

"I love you, too, but what's wrong?" he asked.

"I couldn't hear you. I thought I was losing you." Mallie whispered.

"I told you we were going to be together. Nothing will keep us apart." replied Daniel holding her tighter.

"Daniel," said Mary with tears in her eyes as she came to Daniel's bedside.

Mallie shifted to Daniel's side, but he kept her close in his arms.

They looked around at the group of people in the room with them. Mallie hid her face in Daniel's side. She had not been aware of all of the people in his room. Her only focus had been Daniel. Daniel looked over at a smiling Matt. He smiled back at him.

"Hi, Matt it's good to see you. Congratulations on your engagement."

"It's good to see you awake. How did you know about mine and Barbara's engagement?" asked Matt.

"I heard you talking. I was here I just couldn't communicate," said Daniel.

The doctor stepped to the side of the bed. "I need to check both of you out," he said.

Daniel shook his head. "Forget it Doc. I'm fine and Mallie is fine. We are not going anywhere. You can check us out tomorrow. We have a lot of catching up to do."

The doctor thought about it for a minute. "Well, all of the labs are closed for the night. There is really no problem with waiting. I will have the nurse keep a check on you both. I'll see you in the morning, both of you. If there is any problem, call the nurse."

"Will do, Doc," said Daniel.

After the doctor and the nurses left, Daniel and Mallie looked around.

Mallie saw Dana and Bob looking on, in astonishment.

"Hi, Mom. Hi, Bob, welcome to the family. I'm glad you and Mom are getting together." She gave them both a big smile. She stayed at Daniel's side. There was no way she was letting go of him after almost losing him.

Dana came to the bedside. "Oh Mallie," Dana said with

tears in her eyes. She looked hard at Mallie for a minute. "What little girl?" she demanded.

Mallie looked blank for a minute, then understanding came. "Oh, Mom, is that all you got from all of this? There is no little girl, yet. It's the little girl Daniel promised me after we are married."

"You two are getting married?" asked an astonished Dana, a question that was echoed around the room.

"Of course we are." said Daniel. "We love each other."

"I didn't know that you even knew each other," said Dana.

"We didn't." said Daniel. "We met while we were in the comas."

"How could you meet in a coma?" asked Mary.

"We started communicating with each other because we couldn't get through to anyone else. We have spent the time getting to know each other," said Daniel.

"I am just so thankful to Mallie for bringing you back to us," said a tearful Mary.

"My new little sister is a fighter," said Matt grinning at Mallie.

Katie came forward to Daniel's bed side. She could hardly see through her tears. "Hi, Katie," said Daniel. "It's good to see you and Brian."

"It's good to see you awake," said Katie. "Welcome back." She leaned forward and kissed Daniel's cheek then leaned over further and kissed Mallie's cheek. "Welcome to the family, little sister," she said.

Mallie smiled up at her tearfully. "Thank you, I'm looking forward to meeting Sylvia," she said. Katie beamed at her.

Herman came forward and, leaning down, gave his son a hug. He patted Mallie on the arm. "I love you, son. I'm glad you are with us again."

"I love you too, Dad. I'm glad to be back."

Daniel looked around at the people in the room. They were his family. They were here for him and would always be here for him and Mallie. They were a great group of people.

"I love all of you guys and I want to thank all of you for being here for me and Mallie, but Mallie and I need some rest. Why don't all of you go home and get some rest in your own beds. You can come back tomorrow. We are not going to be here long. No matter what the doctor thinks. I know we have just awakened from comas, but it was not a restful time. We are fine, now, good night everyone.

They all came by to hug or shake hands. Soon, the room was cleared. Daniel looked at Mallie. "I love you."

He pulled her close and they settled for the first night together in a soft bed. They were both sound asleep, soon. They didn't notice when the nurse came in to check on them. She just smiled and left them sleeping. This was one story that would make the rounds at the hospital for years to come. Some people might not believe it, only the ones who believe in Love's Magic.

ABOUT THE AUTHOR

With five children, ten grandchildren and six great- grandchildren I have a very busy life, but reading and writing have always been a very large and enjoyable part of my life. I have been writing since I was very young. I kept notebooks, with my stories in them private. I didn't share them with anyone. They were all hand written because I was unable to type. We lived in the country and I had to do most of my writing at night. My days were busy helping with my brothers and sister. I also helped Mom with the garden and canning food for our family. Even though I was tired, I still managed to get my thoughts down on paper at night.

When I married and began raising my family, I continued writing my stories while helping my children through school and into their own lives and families. My sister was the only one to read my stories. She was very encouraging. When my youngest daughter started college, I decided to go to college myself. I had taken my GED at an earlier date and only had to take a class to pass my college entrance tests. I passed with flying colors and even managed to get a partial scholarship. I took computer classes to learn typing. The english and literature classes helped me to polish my stories.

I found public speaking was not for me. I was much more comfortable with the written word, but researching and writing the speeches was helpful. I could use information to build a story. I still managed to put my own spin on the essays.

I finished college with an associate degree and a 3.4 GPA. I had several awards including Presidents list, Deans list, and Faculty list. The school experience helped me gain more confidence in my writing. I want to thank my English teacher in college for giving me more confidence in my writing by telling me that I had a good imagination. She said I told an interesting story. My daughter, who is a very good writer and has books of her own published, convinced me to have some of my stories published. She self published them for me. The first time I held one of my books in my hands and looked at my name on it as author, I was so proud. They were very well received. This was encouragement enough to convince me to continue writing and publishing. I have been building my library of books written by Betty McLain since then. I also wrote and illustrated several childrens books.

Being able to type my stories opened up a whole new world for me. Having access to a computer helped me to look up anything I needed to know expanded my ability to keep writing my books. Joining Facebook and making friends all over the world expanded my outlook considerably. I was able to understand many different lifestyles and incorporate them in my ideas.

I have heard the saying, watch out what you say and dont make the writer mad, you may end up in a book being eliminated. It is true. All of life is there to stimulate your imagination. It is fun to sit and think about how a thought can be changed to develop a story, and to watch the story develop and come alive in your mind. When I get started the stories almost write themselves, I just have to get all of it down as I think it before it is gone.

I love knowing the stories I have written are being read and enjoyed by others. It is awe inspiring to look at the books and think I wrote that.

I look forward to many more years of putting my stories out there and hope the people reading my books are looking forward to reading them as much.

Printed in Great Britain
by Amazon

18456202R00072